MORE PRAISE FOR BABYMOUSE!

"Sassy, smart . . .
Babymouse is here
to stay."
—The Horn Book Magazine

"Young readers
will happily
fall in line."
—Kirkus Reviews

"The brother-sister creative team hits the mark
with humor, sweetness, and characters so genuine
they can pass for real kids." —Booklist

"Babymouse is spunky, ambitious,
and, at times, a total dweeb."
—School Library Journal

Be sure to read **all** the **BABYMOUSE** books:

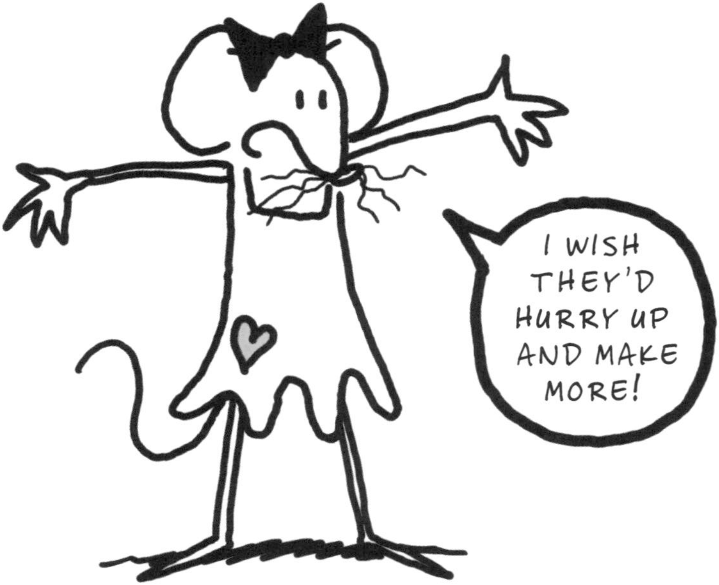
I WISH THEY'D HURRY UP AND MAKE MORE!

BABYMOUSE
ROCK STAR

BY JENNIFER L. HOLM & MATTHEW HOLM

RANDOM HOUSE 🏠 NEW YORK

Copyright © 2006 by Jennifer Holm and Matthew Holm.

All rights reserved.
Published in the United States by Random House Children's Books, a division of Random House, Inc., New York.

RANDOM HOUSE and colophon are registered trademarks of Random House, Inc.

www.randomhouse.com/kids
www.babymouse.com

Educators and librarians, for a variety of teaching tools, visit us at www.randomhouse.com/teachers

Library of Congress Cataloging-in-Publication Data
Holm, Jennifer L.
Babymouse : rock star / Jennifer Holm and Matthew Holm.
    p. cm.
ISBN 978-0-375-83232-1 (trade) — ISBN 978-0-375-93232-8 (lib. bdg.)
I. Graphic novels. I. Holm, Matthew. II. Title.
PN6727.H592B34 2006
741.5'973—dc22
2005046464

MANUFACTURED IN MALAYSIA

14 13 12 11 10 9 8 7 6

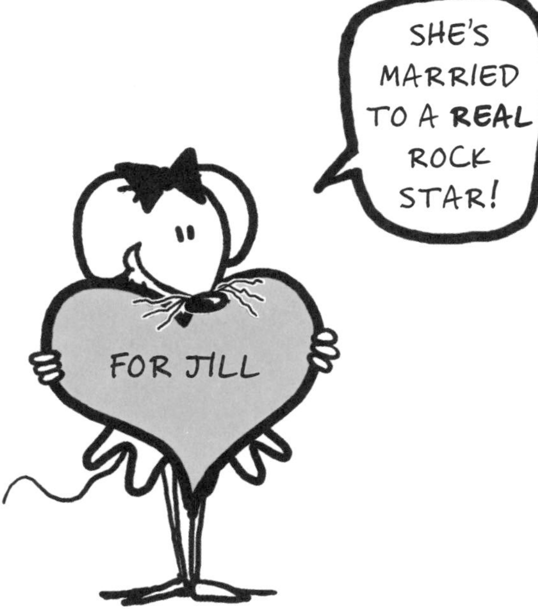
SHE'S MARRIED TO A **REAL** ROCK STAR!
FOR JILL

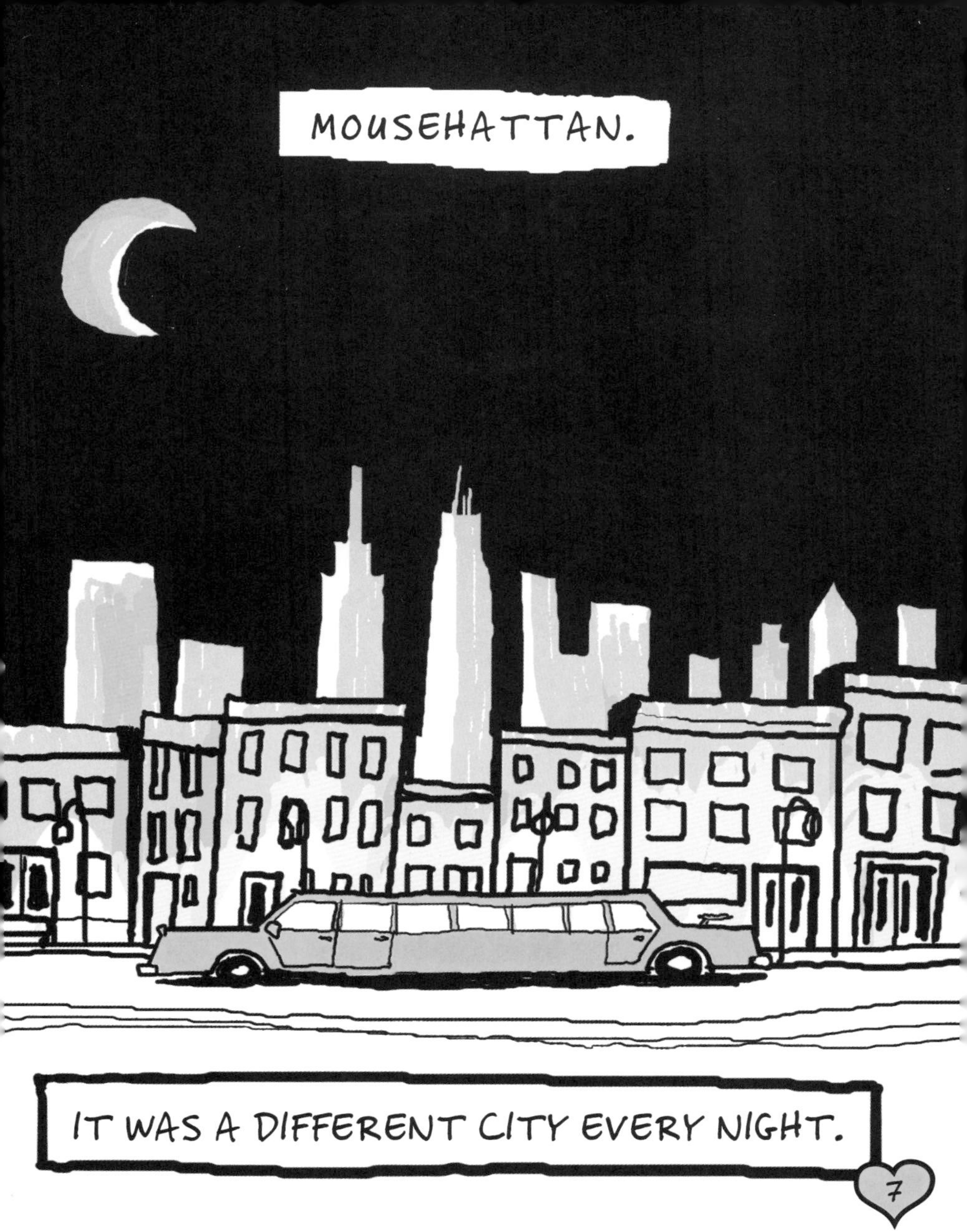
MOUSEHATTAN.
IT WAS A DIFFERENT CITY EVERY NIGHT.

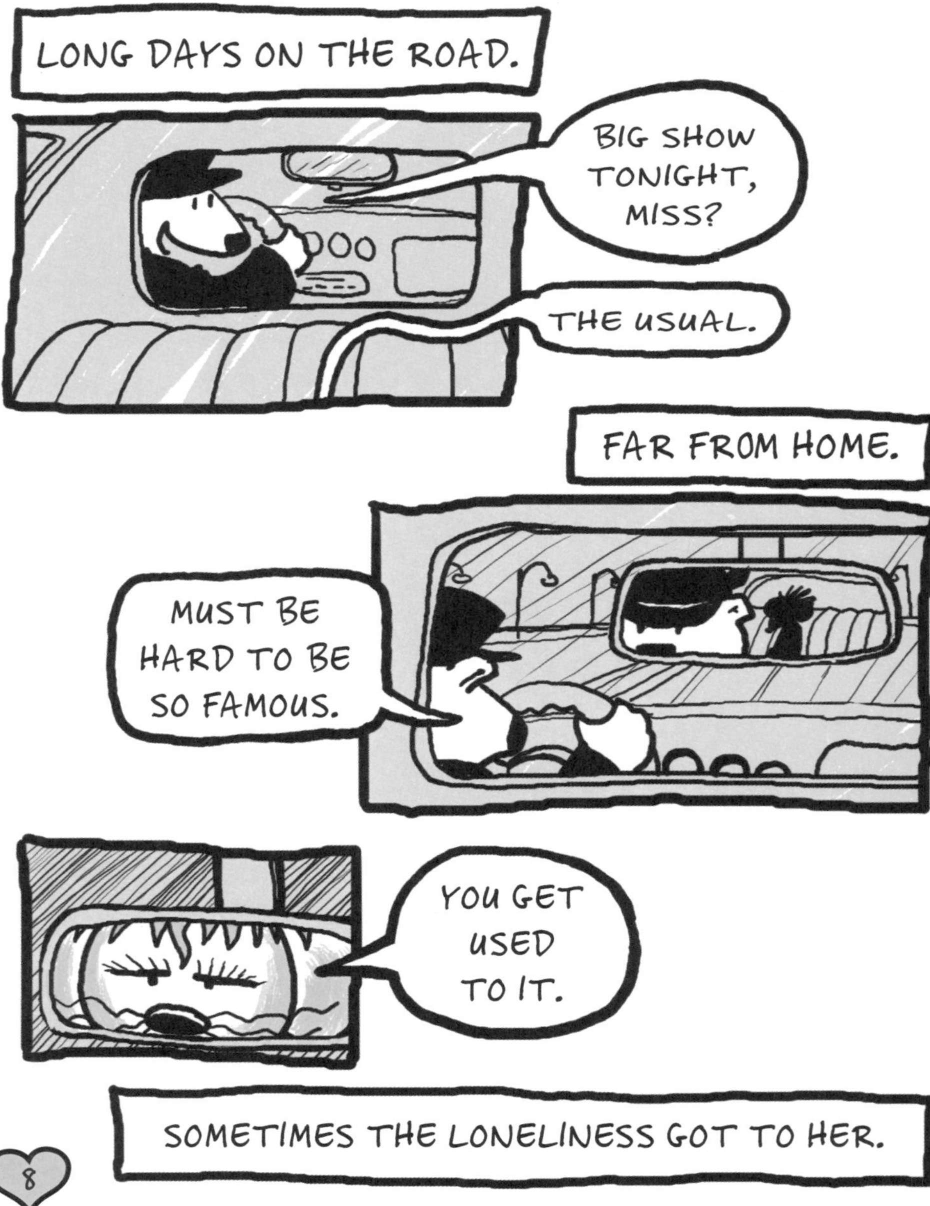
LONG DAYS ON THE ROAD.
BIG SHOW TONIGHT, MISS?
THE USUAL.
FAR FROM HOME.
MUST BE HARD TO BE SO FAMOUS.
YOU GET USED TO IT.
SOMETIMES THE LONELINESS GOT TO HER.

BUT IT WAS THE LIFE SHE HAD CHOSEN.

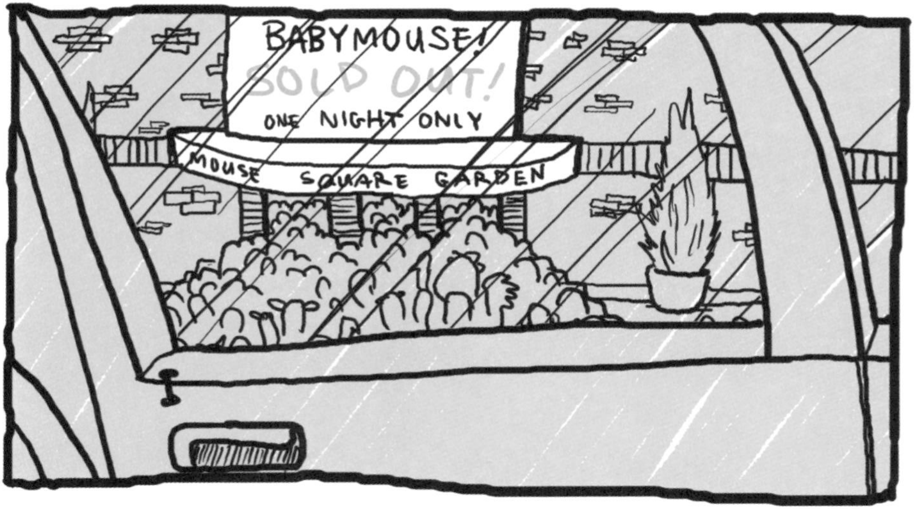
BABYMOUSE!
SOLD OUT!
ONE NIGHT ONLY
MOUSE SQUARE GARDEN

THE ONLY LIFE SHE KNEW.

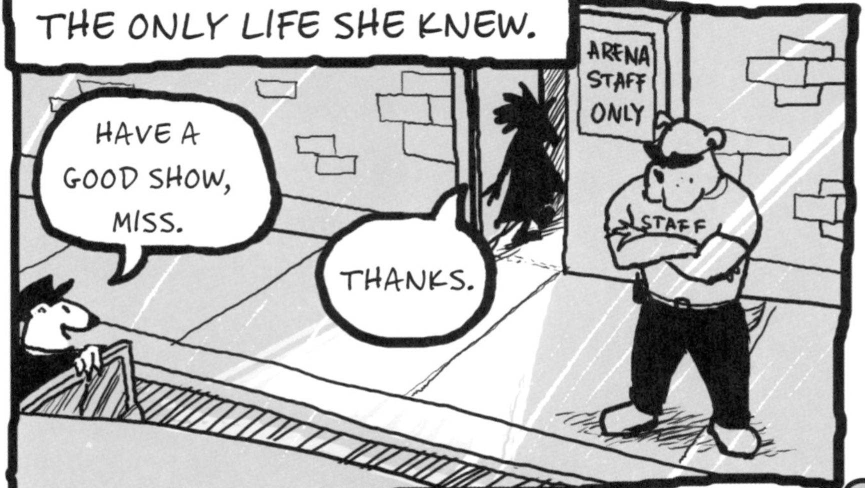
ARENA STAFF ONLY
HAVE A GOOD SHOW, MISS.
THANKS.
STAFF

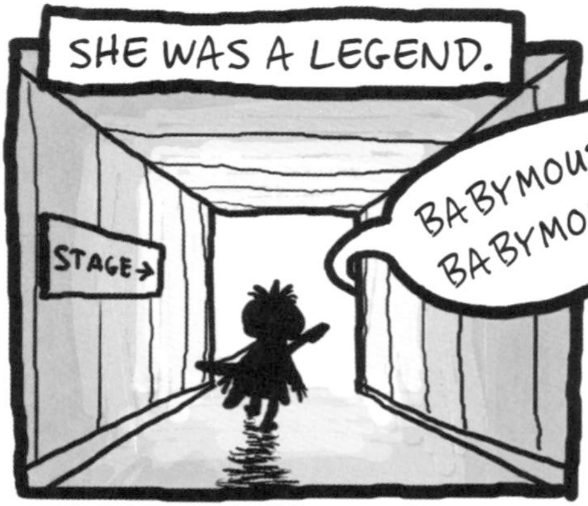
SHE WAS A LEGEND.
STAGE →
BABYMOUSE! BABYMOUSE!

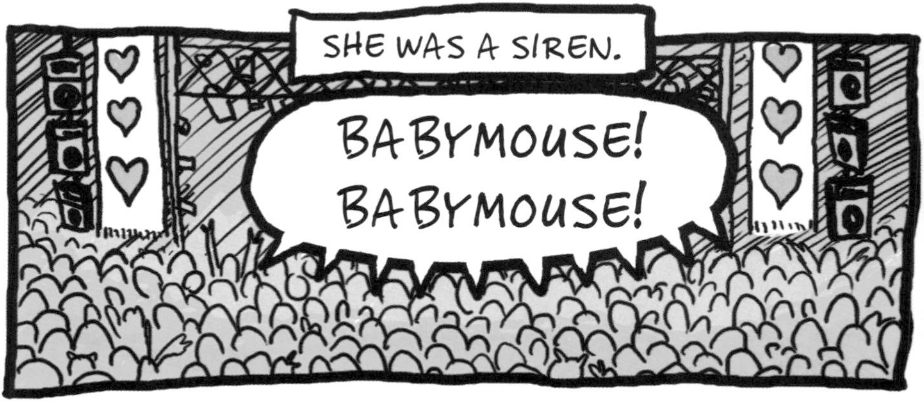
SHE WAS A SIREN.
BABYMOUSE! BABYMOUSE!

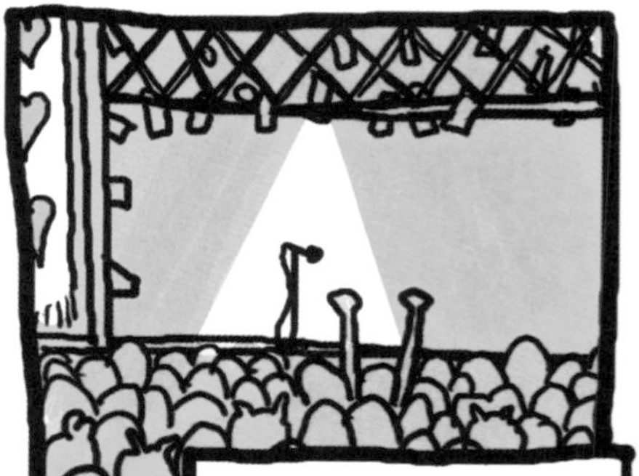
SHE WAS A . . .

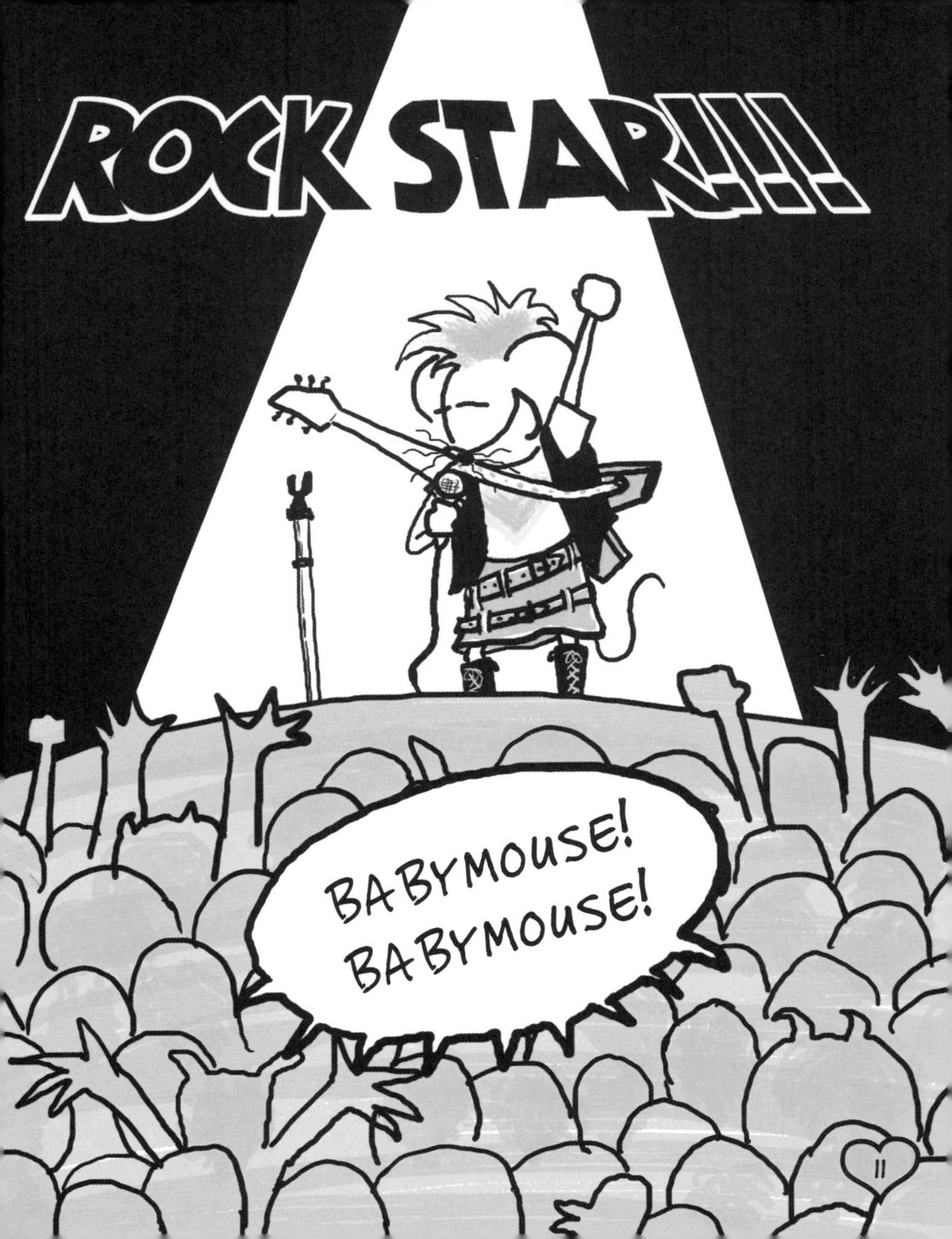
ROCK STAR!!!!
BABYMOUSE! BABYMOUSE!
11

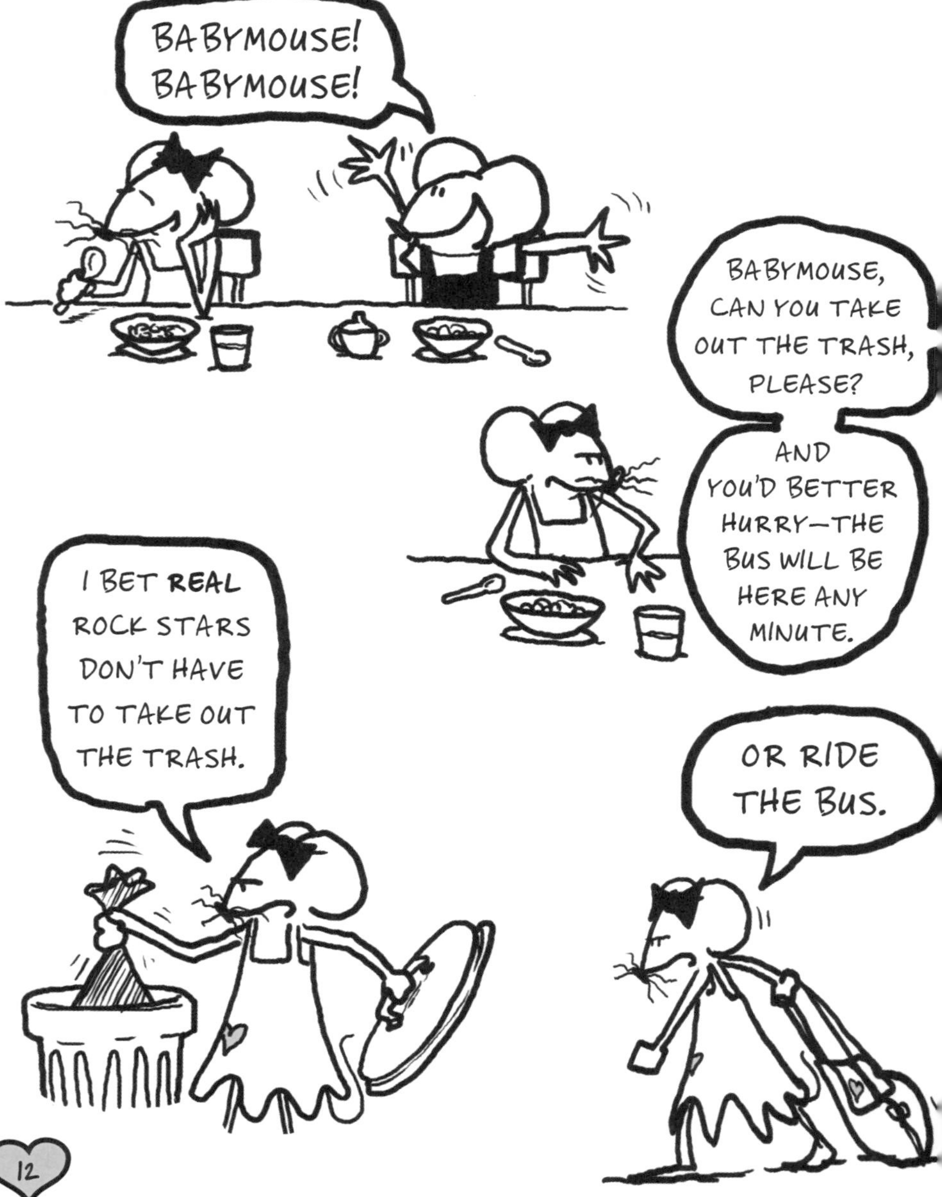
BABYMOUSE! BABYMOUSE!
BABYMOUSE, CAN YOU TAKE OUT THE TRASH, PLEASE?
AND YOU'D BETTER HURRY—THE BUS WILL BE HERE ANY MINUTE.
I BET **REAL** ROCK STARS DON'T HAVE TO TAKE OUT THE TRASH.
OR RIDE THE BUS.

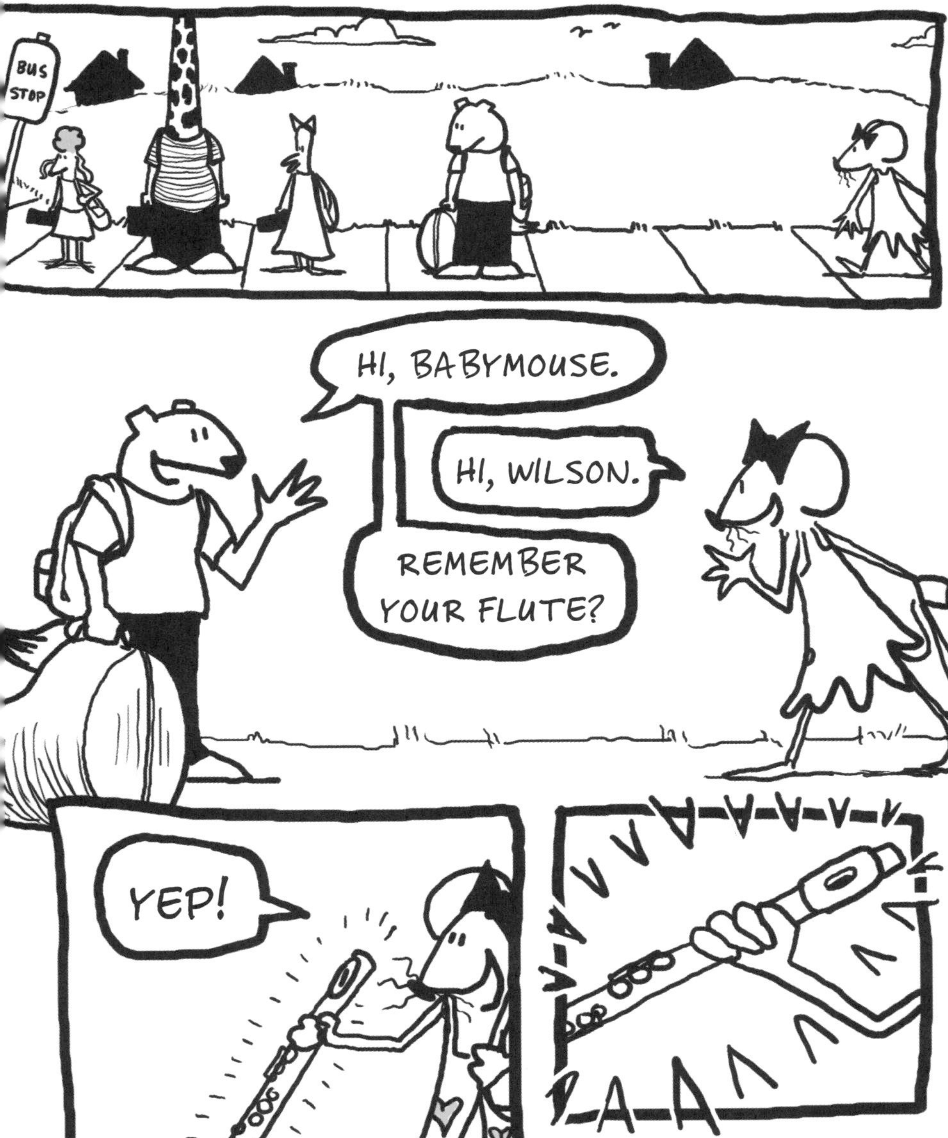
BUS STOP
HI, BABYMOUSE.
HI, WILSON.
REMEMBER YOUR FLUTE?
YEP!
VVVVVV-A-A-A-A-A-V-V-V-A-A-A

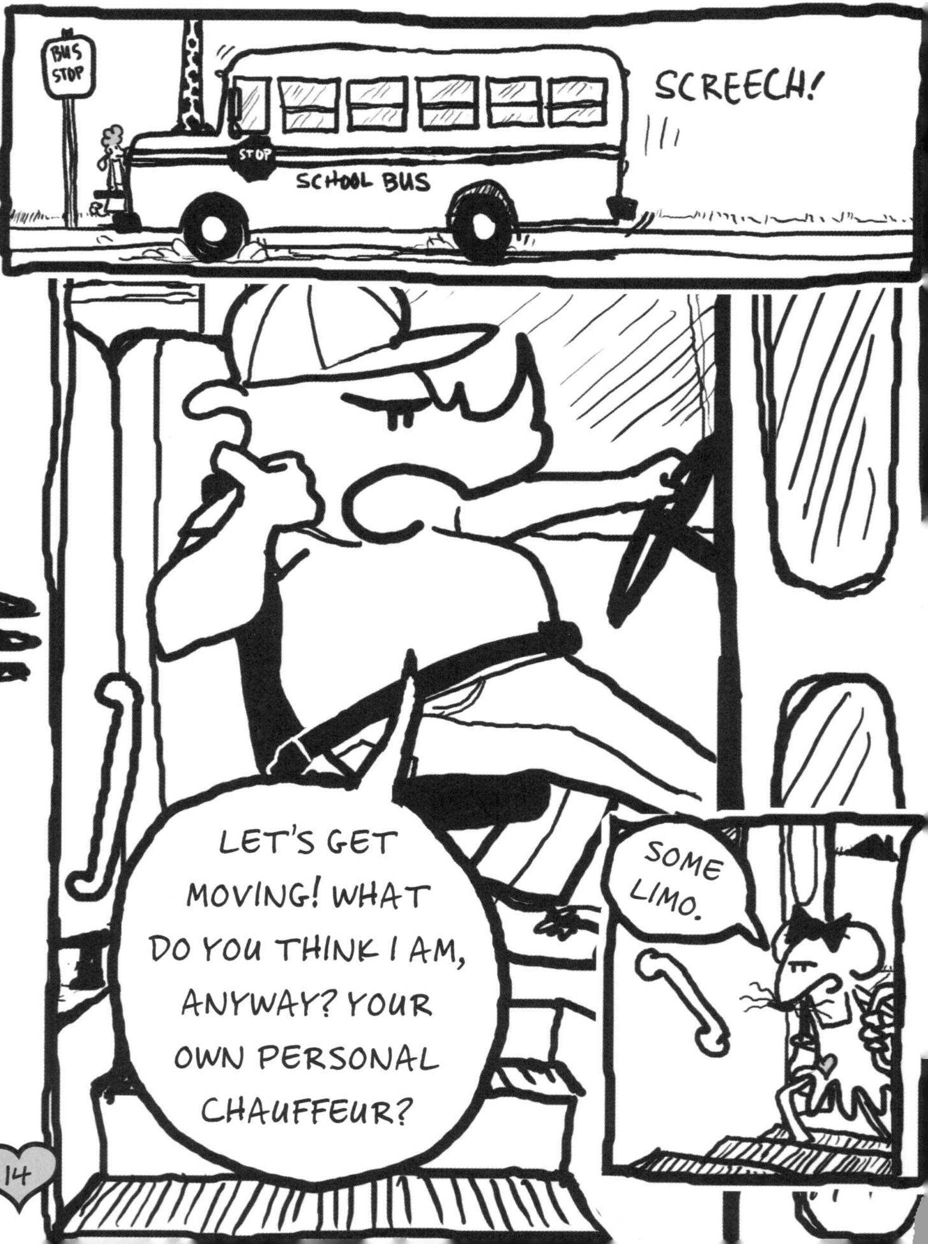
BUS STOP
STOP
SCHOOL BUS
SCREECH!
LET'S GET MOVING! WHAT DO YOU THINK I AM, ANYWAY? YOUR OWN PERSONAL CHAUFFEUR?
SOME LIMO.

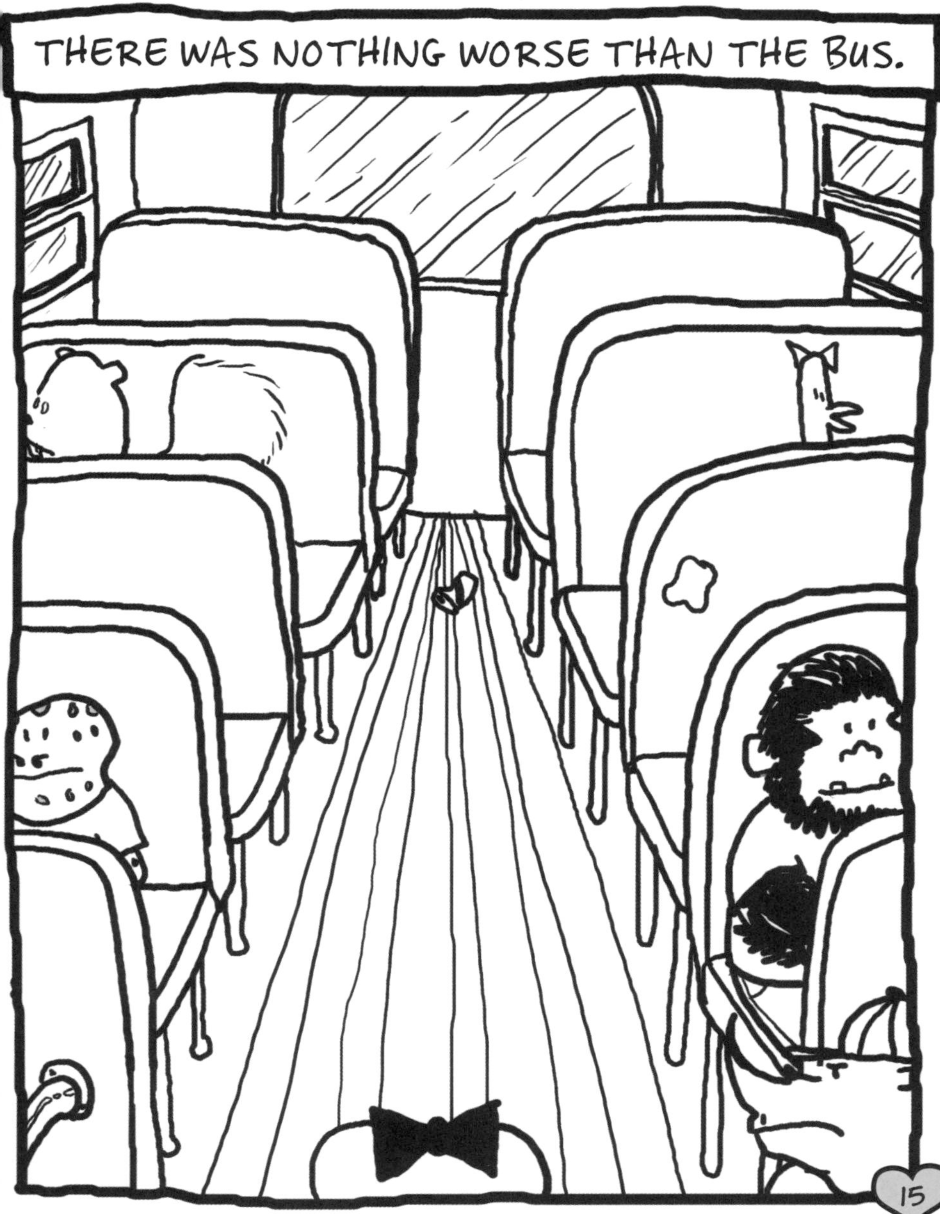
THERE WAS NOTHING WORSE THAN THE BUS.

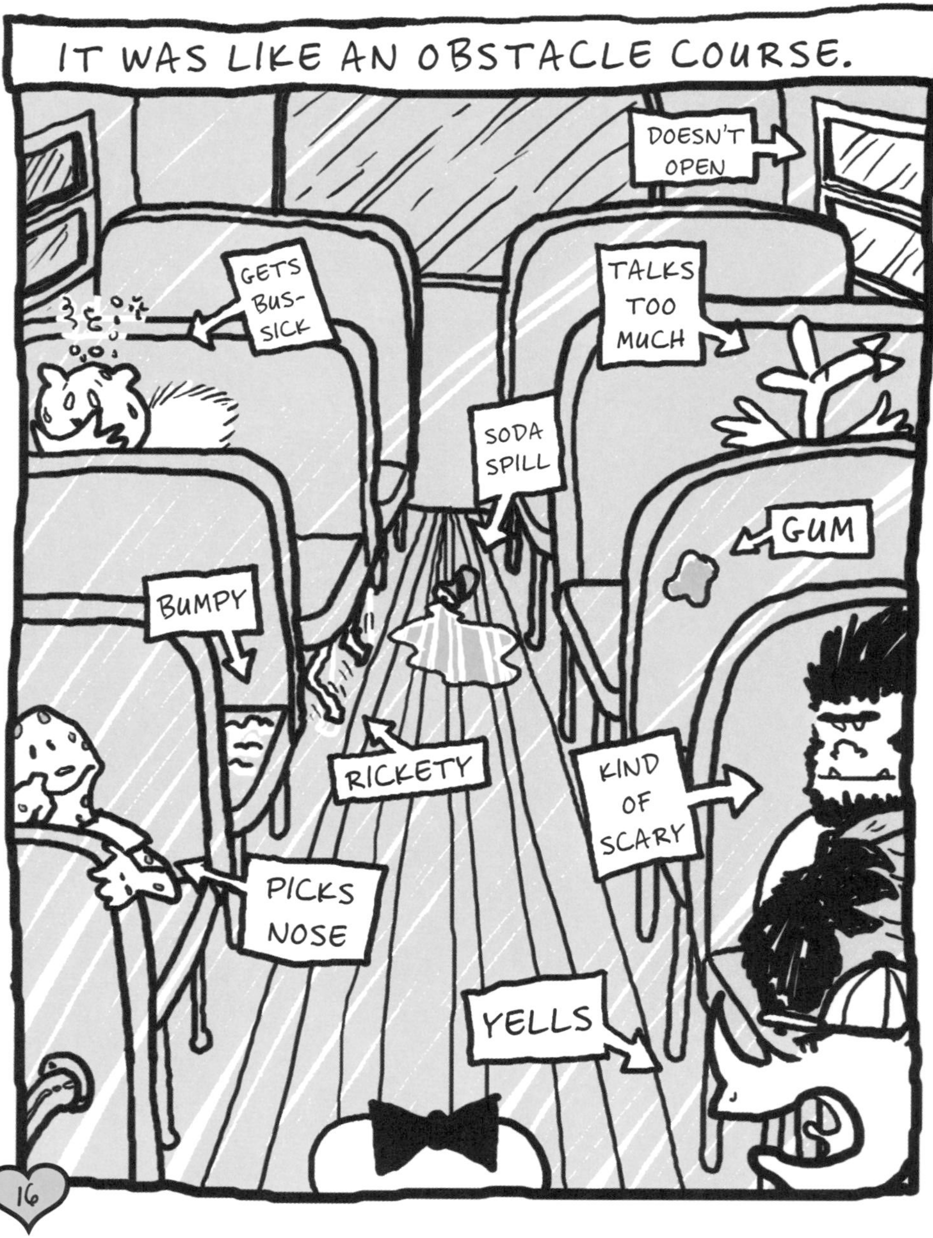
IT WAS LIKE AN OBSTACLE COURSE.
DOESN'T OPEN
GETS BUS-SICK
TALKS TOO MUCH
SODA SPILL
GUM
BUMPY
RICKETY
KIND OF SCARY
PICKS NOSE
YELLS

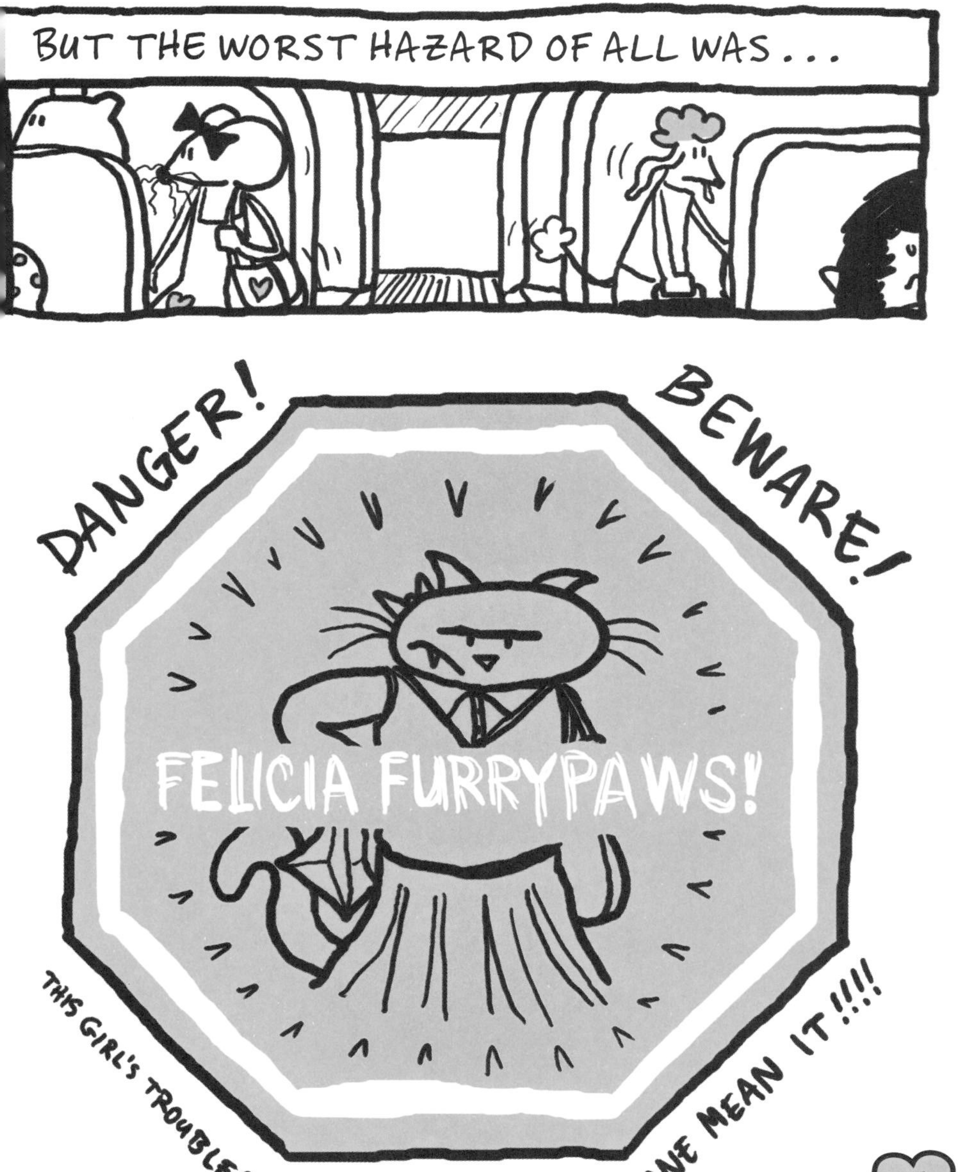
BUT THE WORST HAZARD OF ALL WAS . . .
DANGER!
BEWARE!
FELICIA FURRYPAWS!
THIS GIRL'S TROUBLE!
WE MEAN IT!!!!

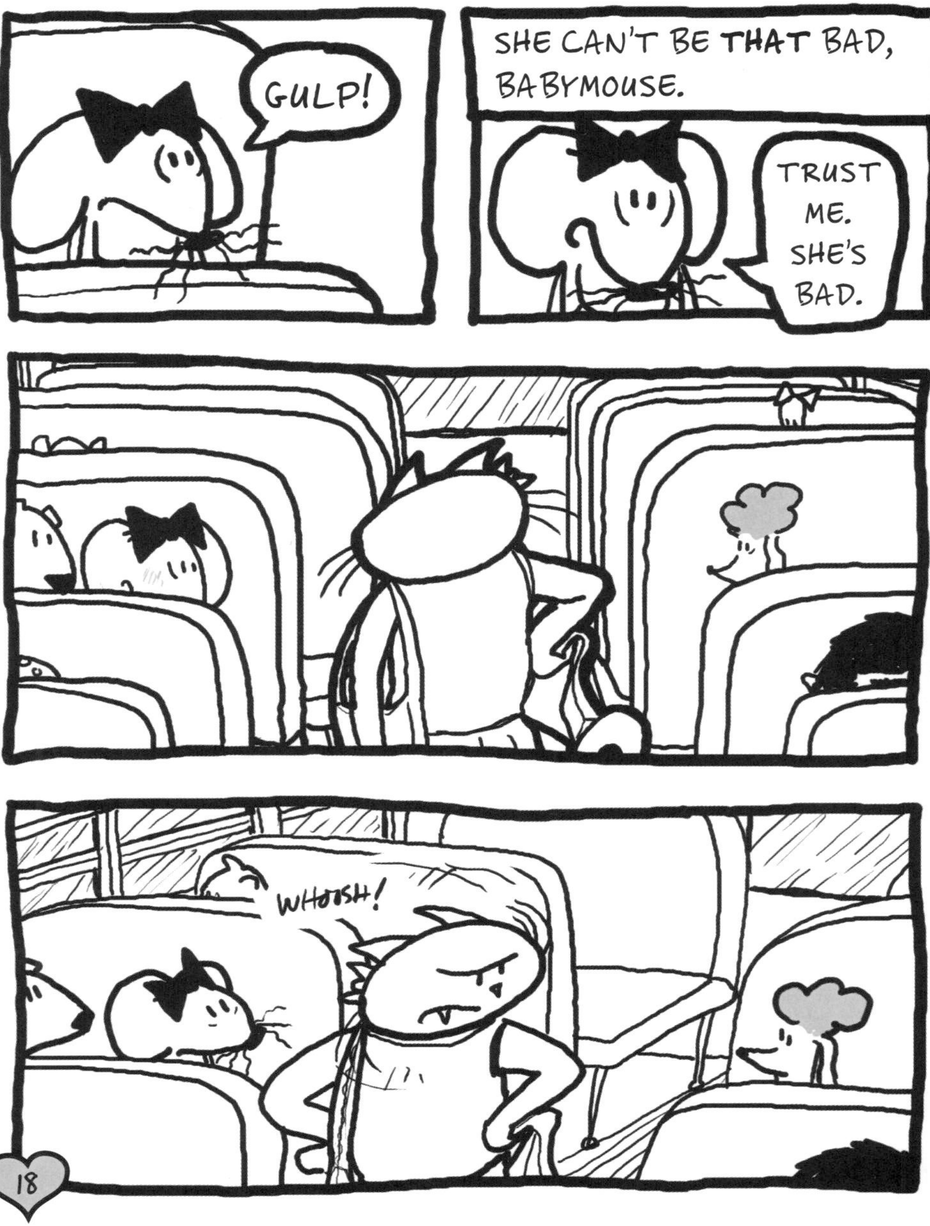
GULP!
SHE CAN'T BE THAT BAD, BABYMOUSE.
TRUST ME. SHE'S BAD.
WHOOSH!

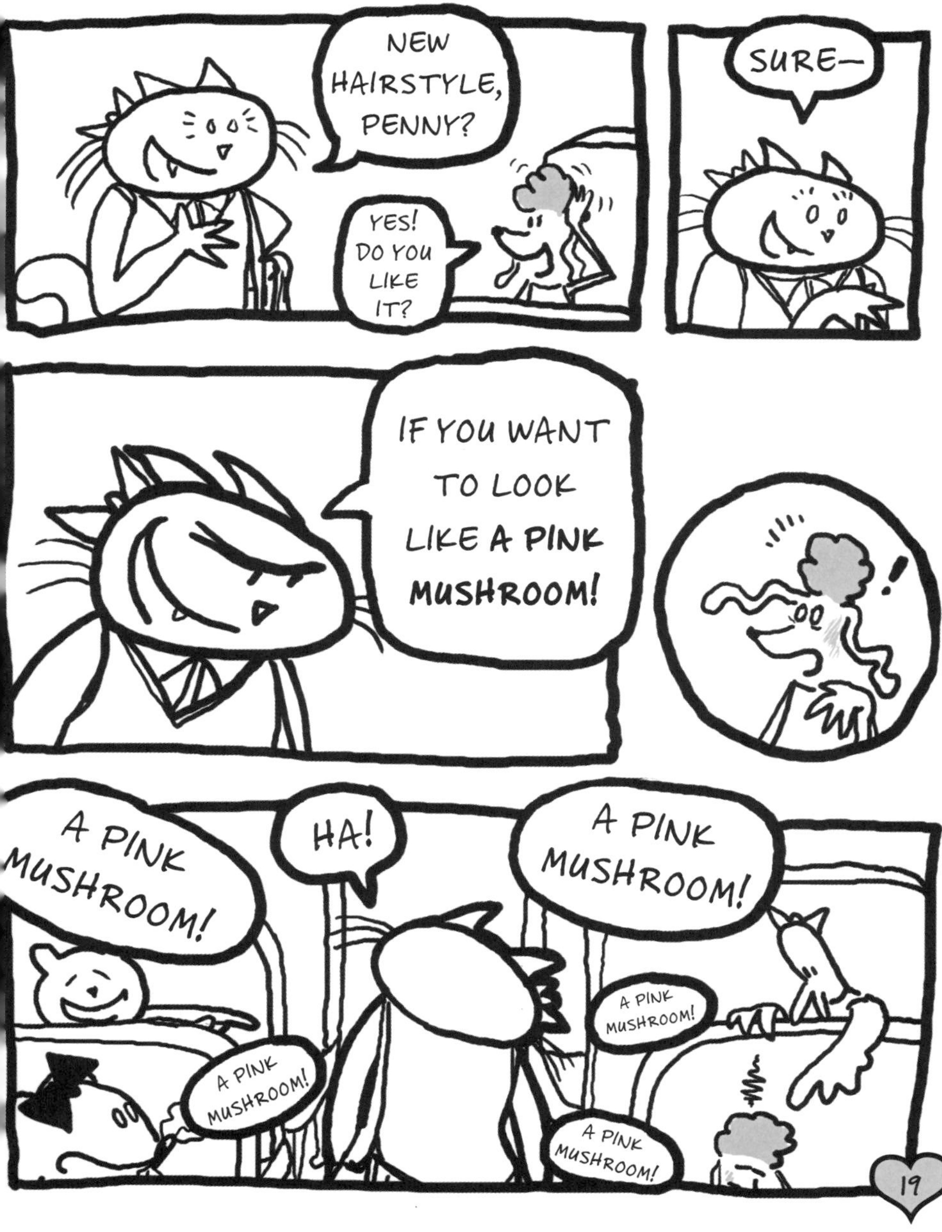
NEW HAIRSTYLE, PENNY?
YES! DO YOU LIKE IT?
SURE—
IF YOU WANT TO LOOK LIKE A PINK MUSHROOM!
!
A PINK MUSHROOM!
HA!
A PINK MUSHROOM!
A PINK MUSHROOM!
A PINK MUSHROOM!
A PINK MUSHROOM!

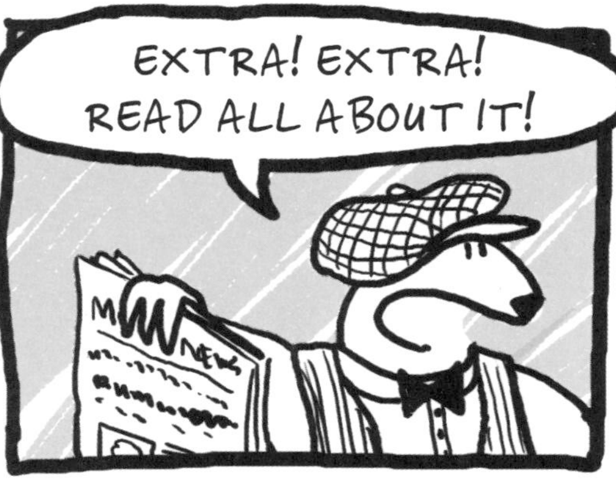
EXTRA! EXTRA! READ ALL ABOUT IT!

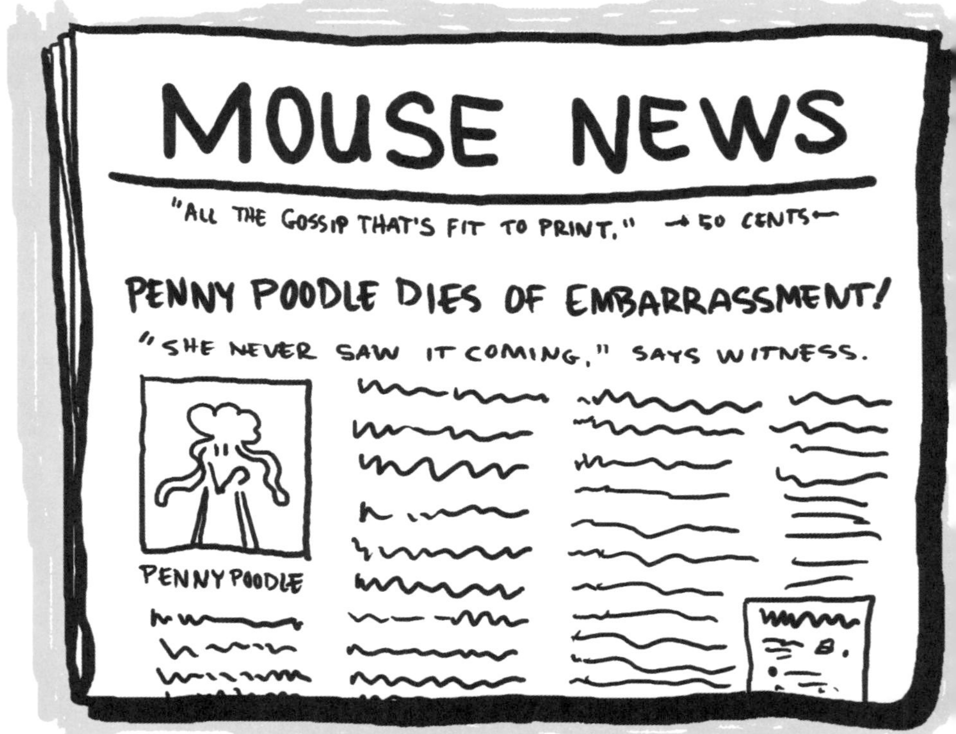
MOUSE NEWS
"ALL THE GOSSIP THAT'S FIT TO PRINT."
50 CENTS
PENNY POODLE DIES OF EMBARRASSMENT!
"SHE NEVER SAW IT COMING," SAYS WITNESS.
PENNY POODLE

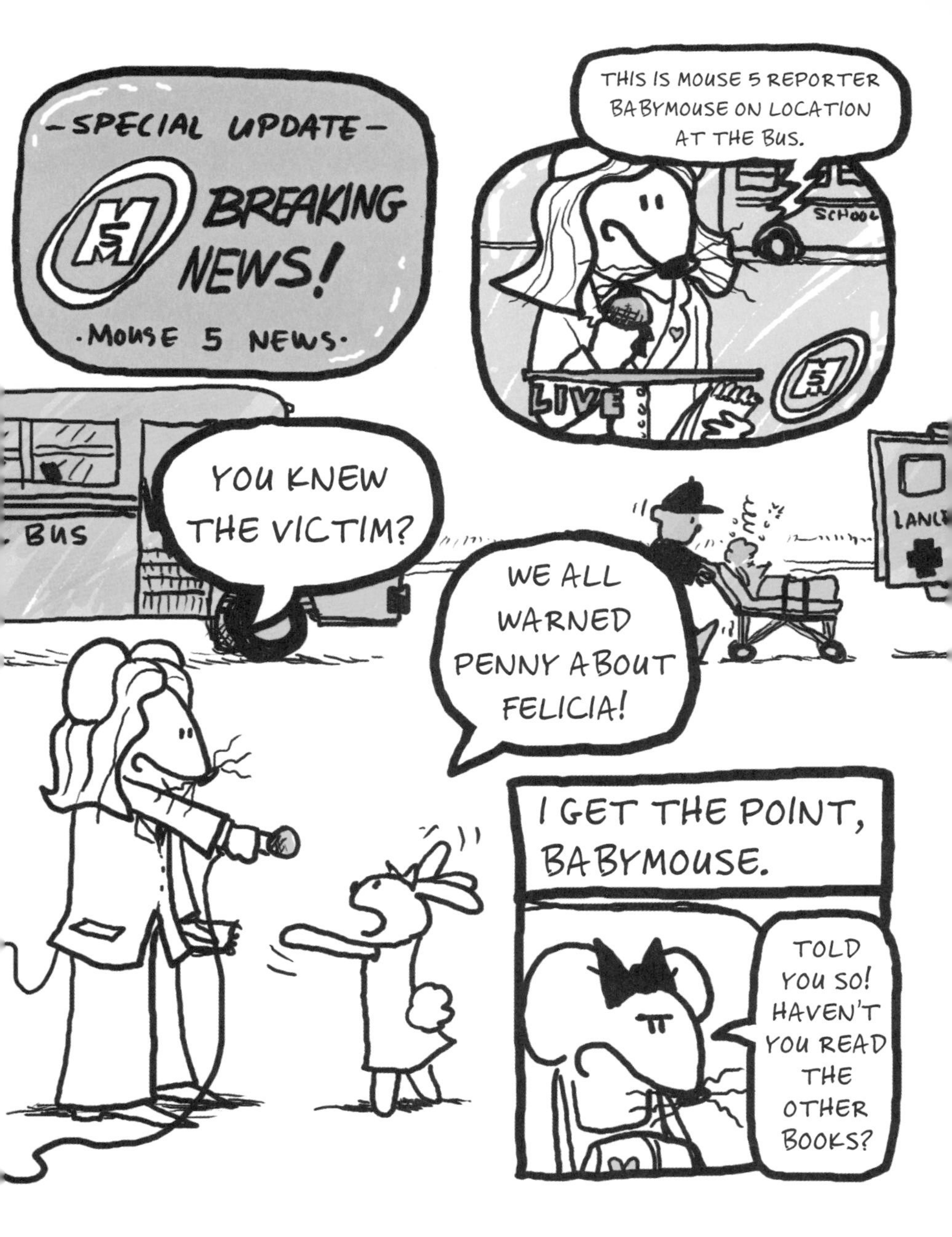

-SPECIAL UPDATE-
BREAKING NEWS!
·MOUSE 5 NEWS·
THIS IS MOUSE 5 REPORTER BABYMOUSE ON LOCATION AT THE BUS.
SCHOOL
LIVE
BUS
YOU KNEW THE VICTIM?
WE ALL WARNED PENNY ABOUT FELICIA!
I GET THE POINT, BABYMOUSE.
TOLD YOU SO! HAVEN'T YOU READ THE OTHER BOOKS?

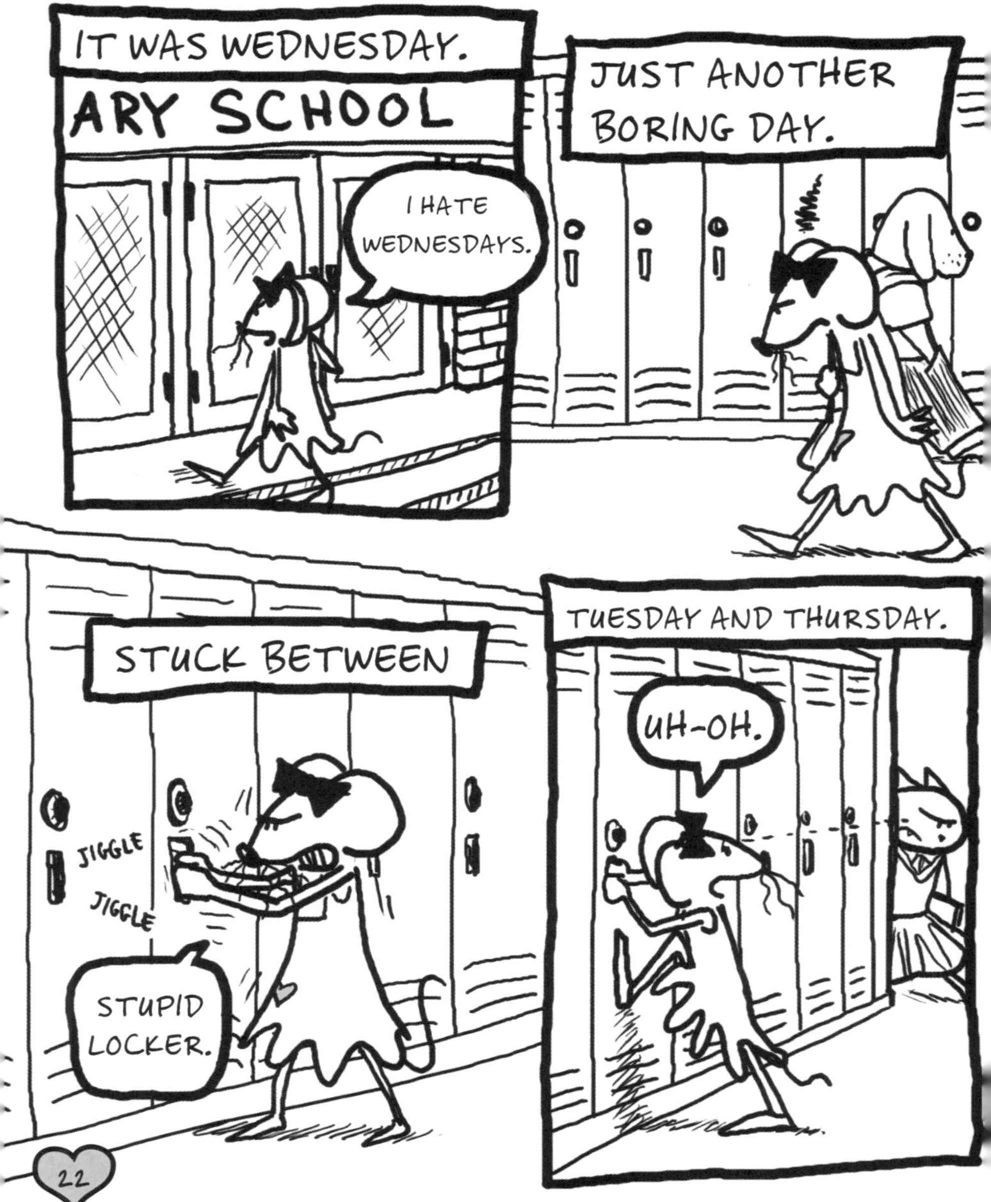
IT WAS WEDNESDAY.
ARY SCHOOL
I HATE WEDNESDAYS.
JUST ANOTHER BORING DAY.
STUCK BETWEEN
JIGGLE
JIGGLE
STUPID LOCKER.
TUESDAY AND THURSDAY.
UH-OH.

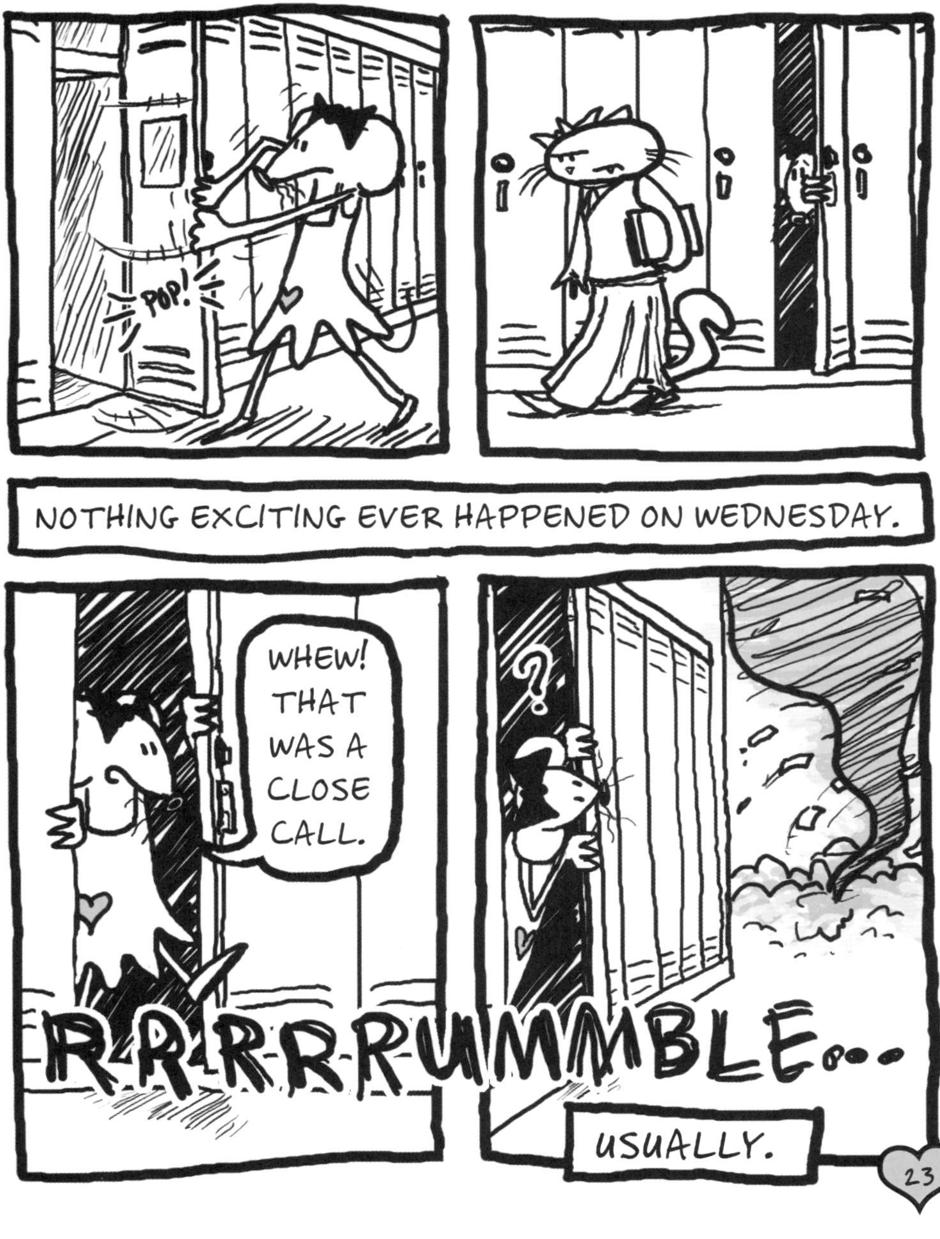
POP!
NOTHING EXCITING EVER HAPPENED ON WEDNESDAY.
WHEW! THAT WAS A CLOSE CALL.
?
RRRRRRUMMMBLE...
USUALLY.

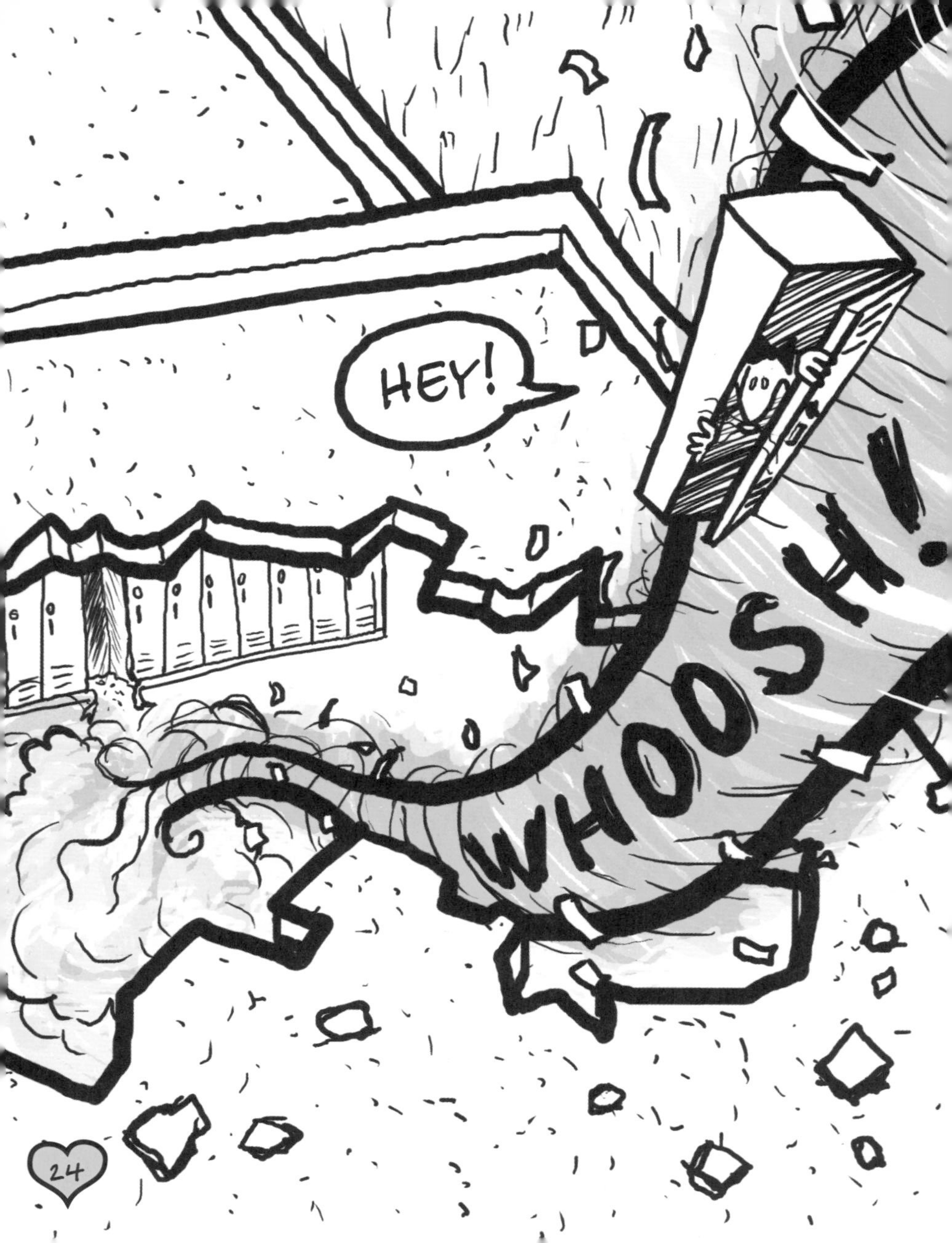
HEY!
WHOOSH!

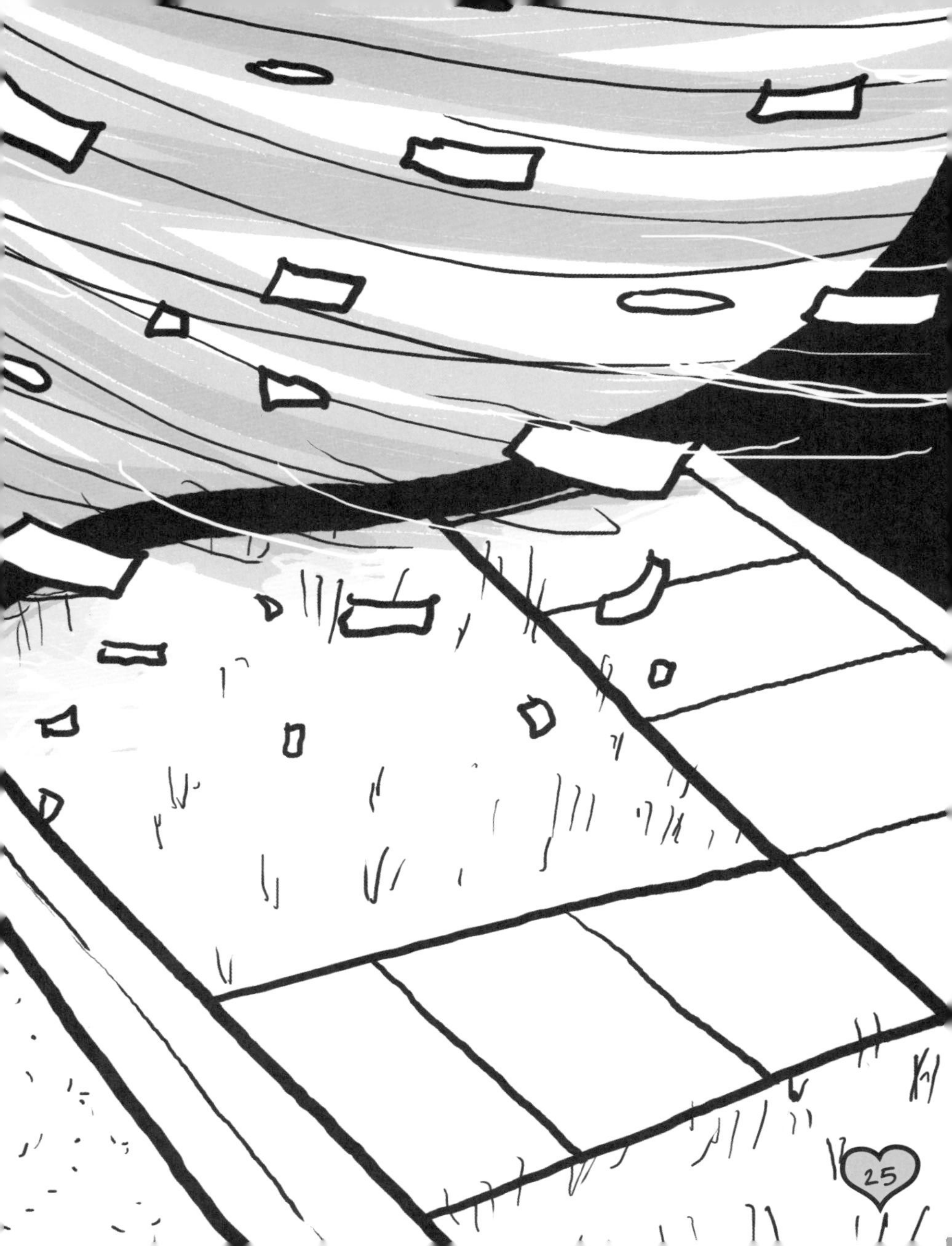

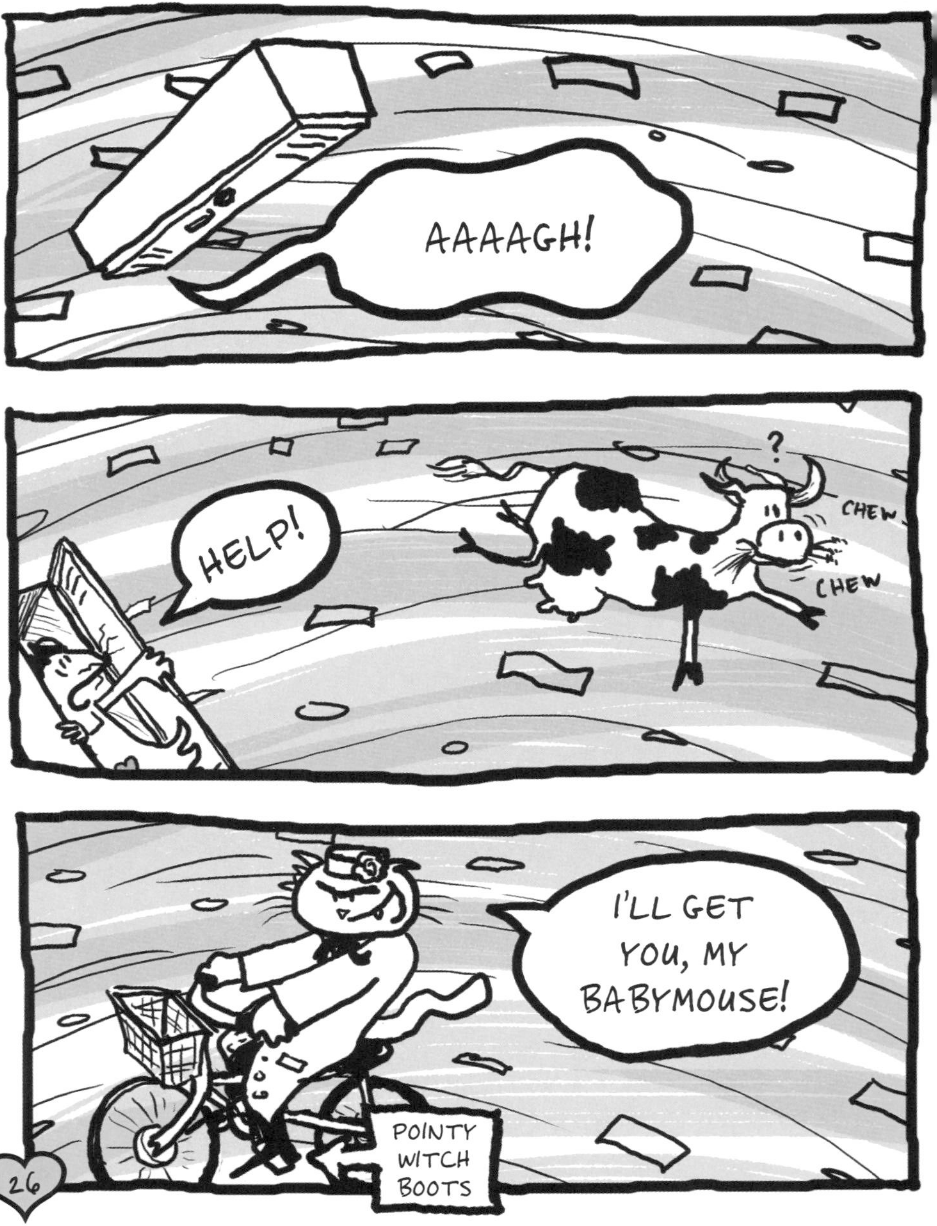
AAAAGH!
HELP!
?
CHEW
CHEW
I'LL GET YOU, MY BABYMOUSE!
POINTY WITCH BOOTS

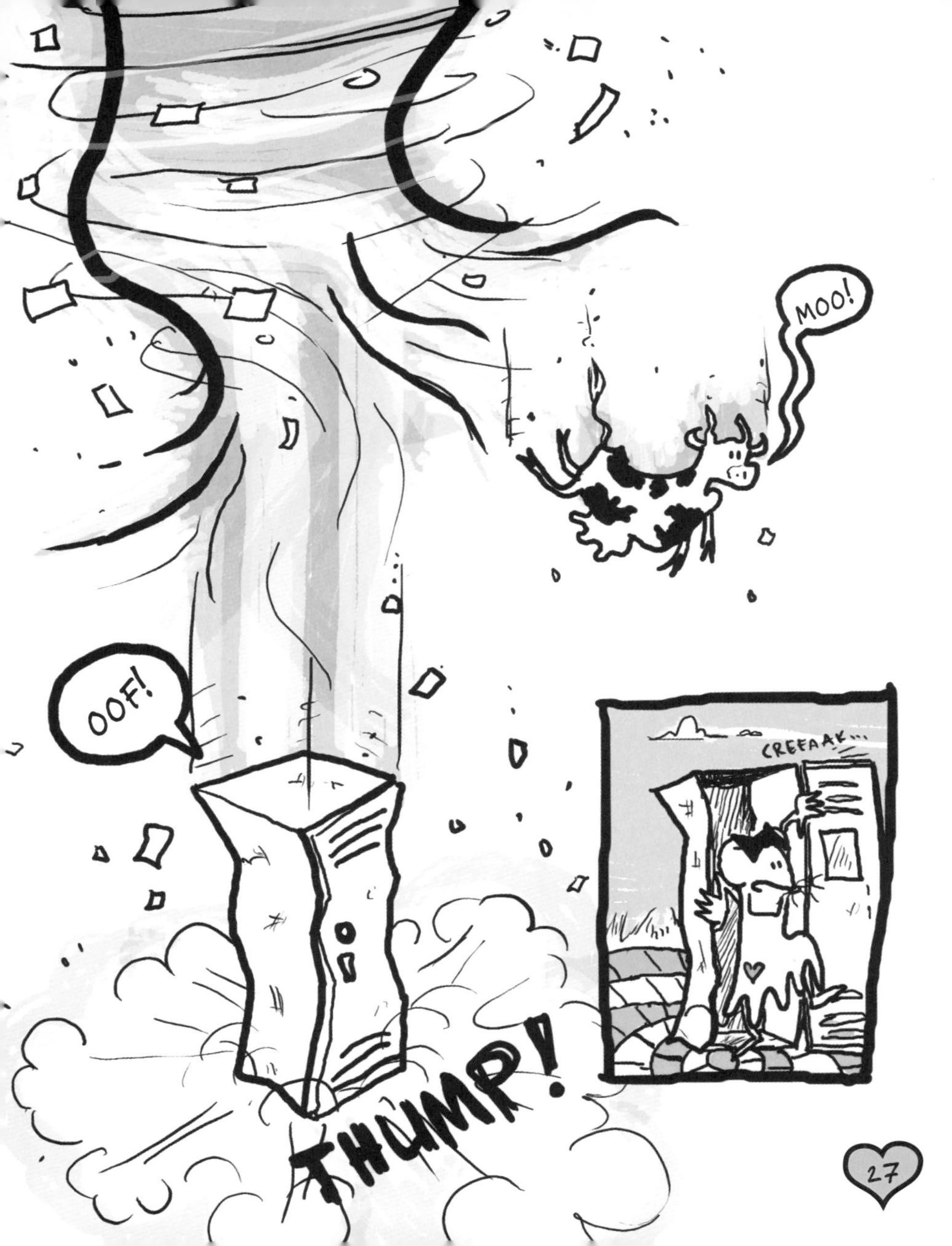
MOO!
OOF!
THUMP!
CREEAAK...

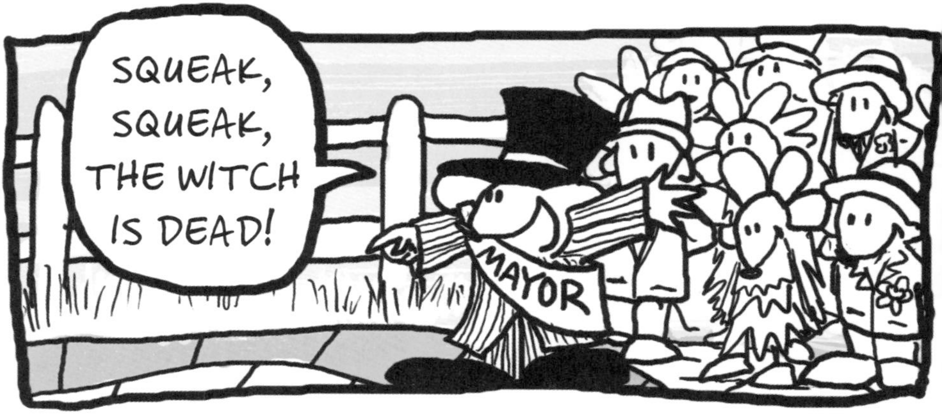
SQUEAK, SQUEAK, THE WITCH IS DEAD!
MAYOR

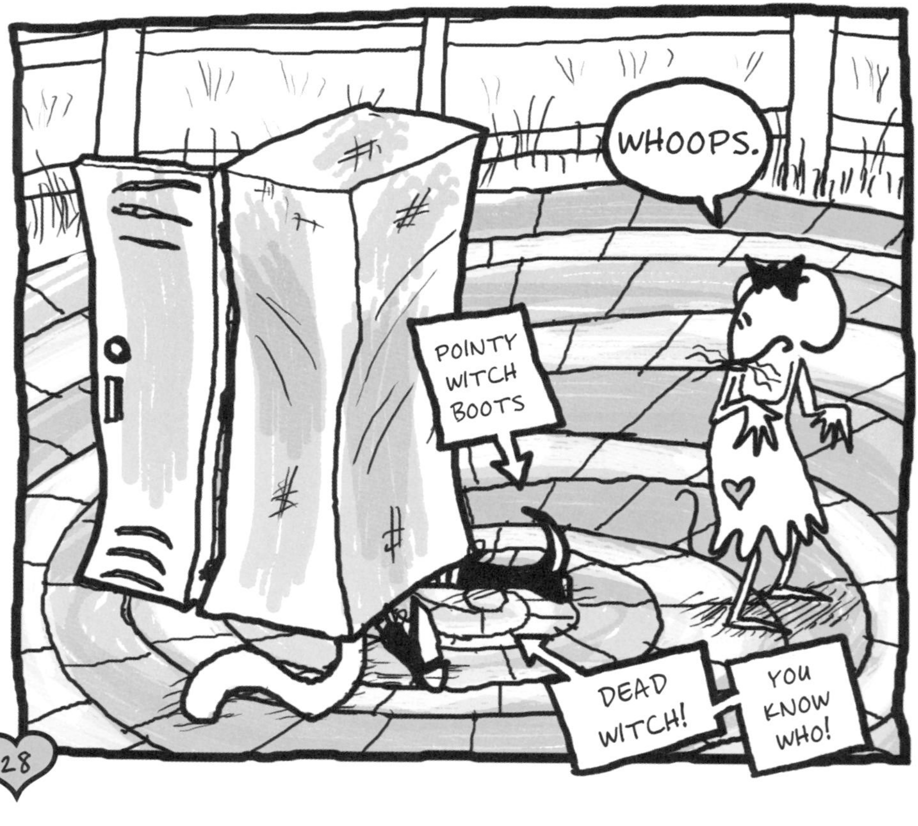
WHOOPS.
POINTY WITCH BOOTS
DEAD WITCH!
YOU KNOW WHO!

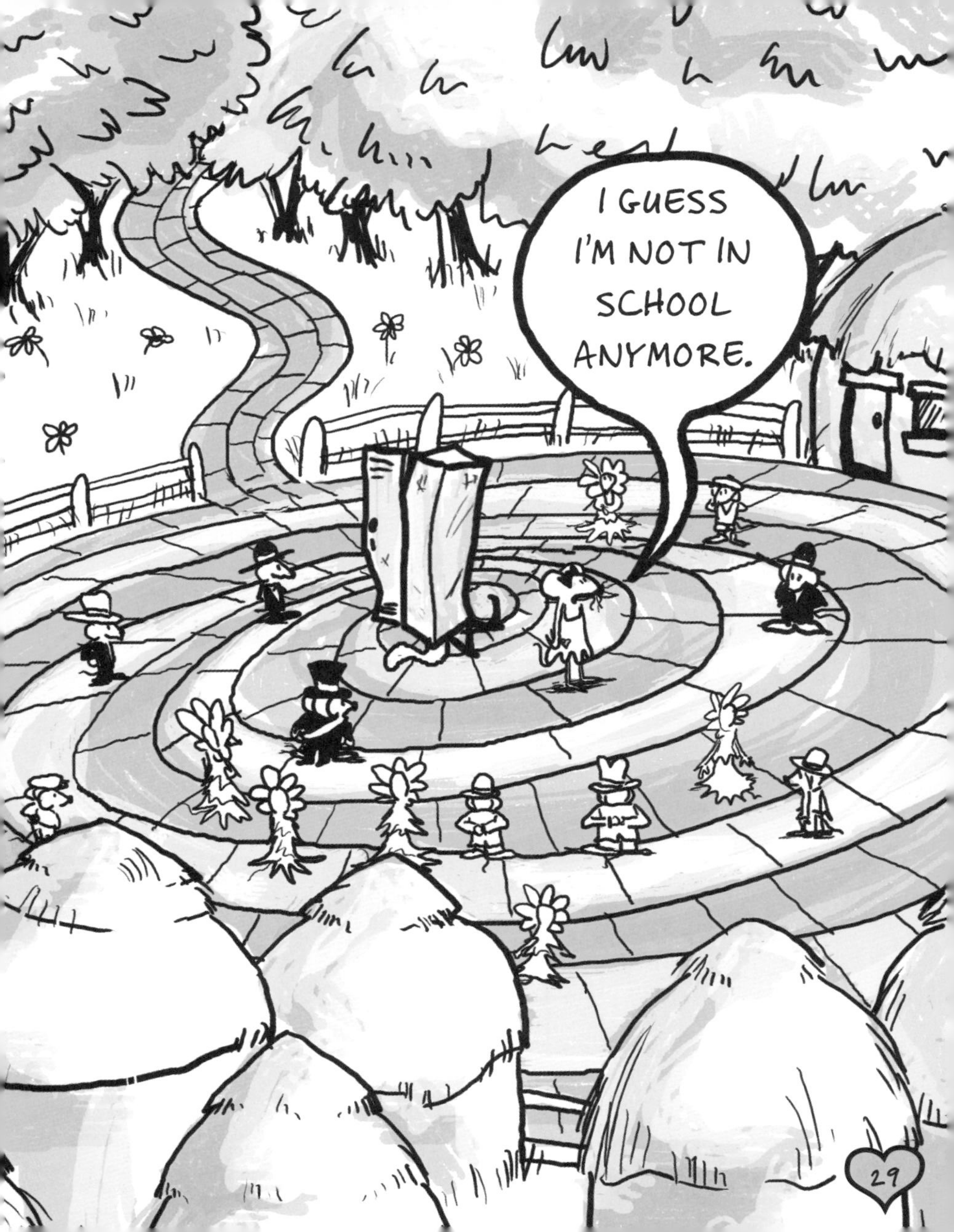
I GUESS I'M NOT IN SCHOOL ANYMORE.

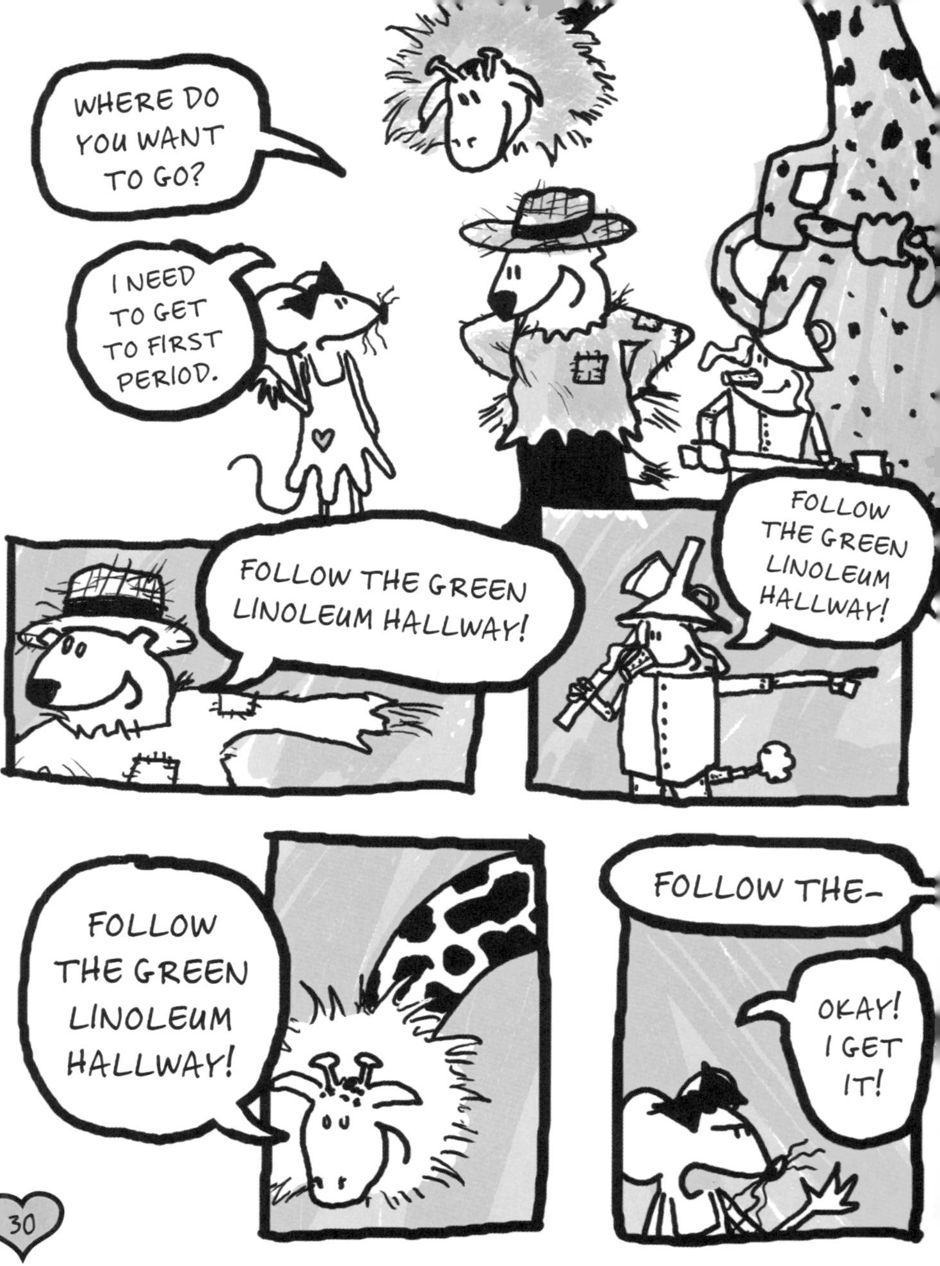
WHERE DO YOU WANT TO GO?
I NEED TO GET TO FIRST PERIOD.
FOLLOW THE GREEN LINOLEUM HALLWAY!
FOLLOW THE GREEN LINOLEUM HALLWAY!
FOLLOW THE GREEN LINOLEUM HALLWAY!
FOLLOW THE–
OKAY! I GET IT!

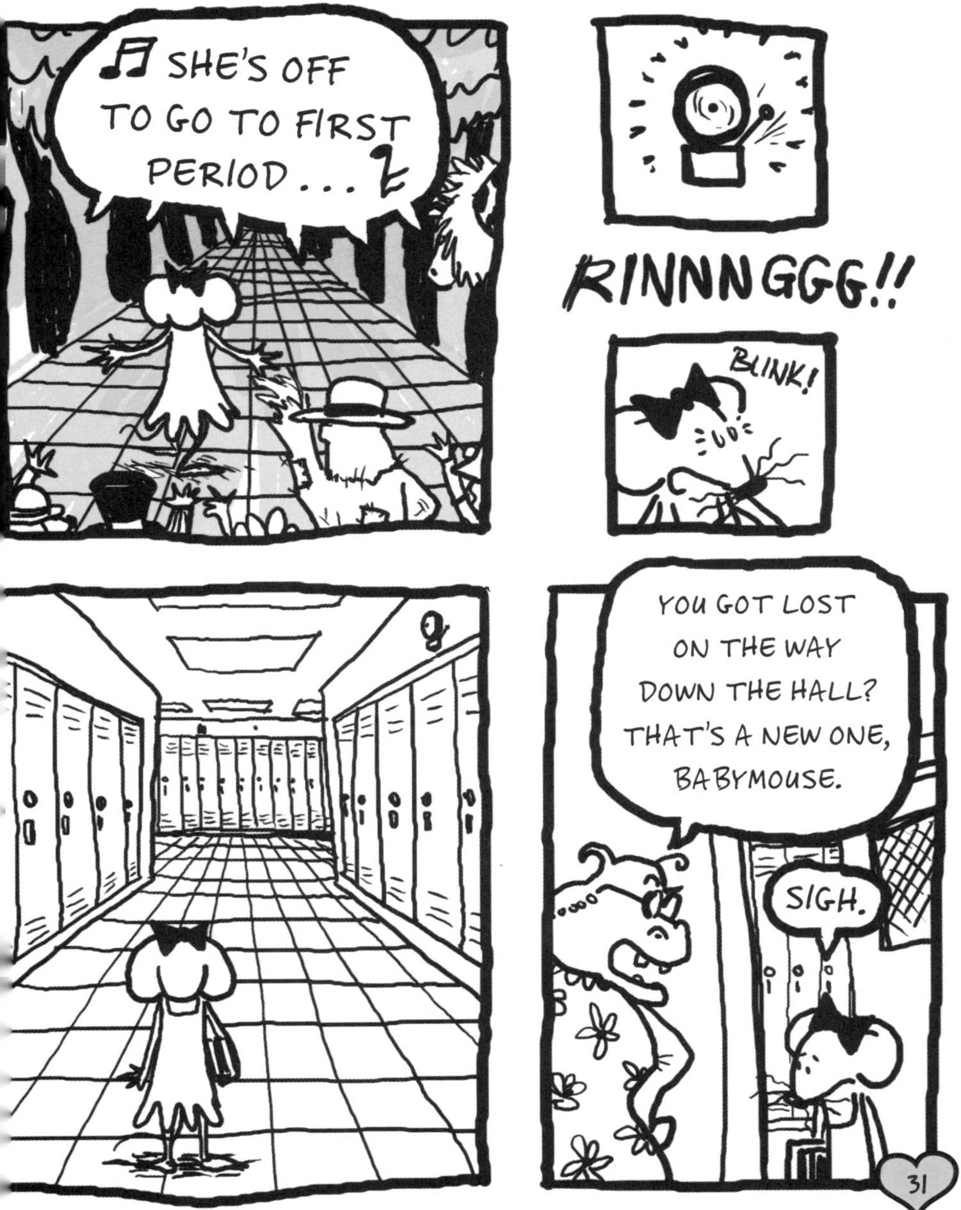
♫ SHE'S OFF TO GO TO FIRST PERIOD... ♪
RINNNGGG!!
BLINK!
YOU GOT LOST ON THE WAY DOWN THE HALL? THAT'S A NEW ONE, BABYMOUSE.
SIGH.

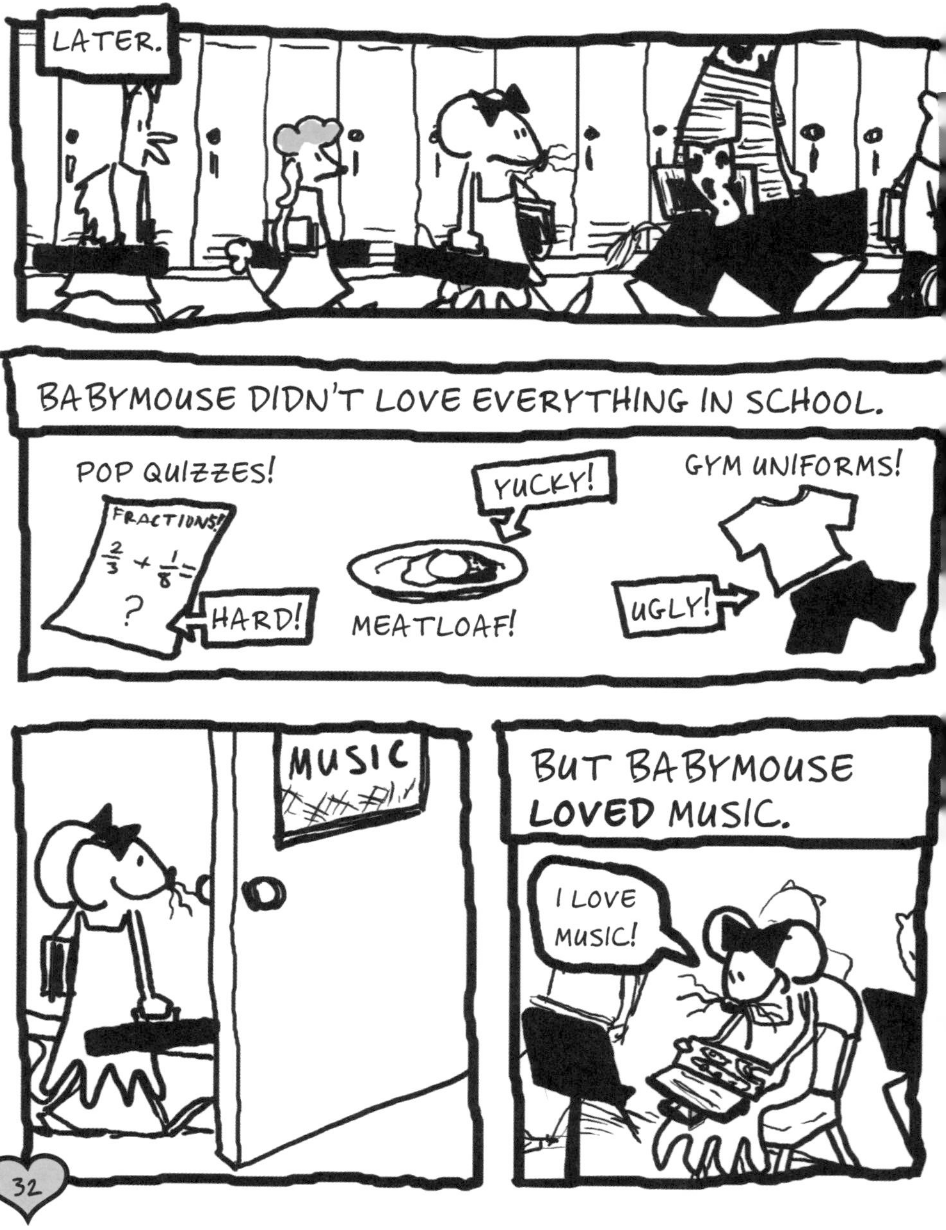

LATER.
BABYMOUSE DIDN'T LOVE EVERYTHING IN SCHOOL.
POP QUIZZES!
FRACTIONS!
2/3 + 1/8 =
?
HARD!
YUCKY!
MEATLOAF!
GYM UNIFORMS!
UGLY!
MUSIC
BUT BABYMOUSE LOVED MUSIC.
I LOVE MUSIC!

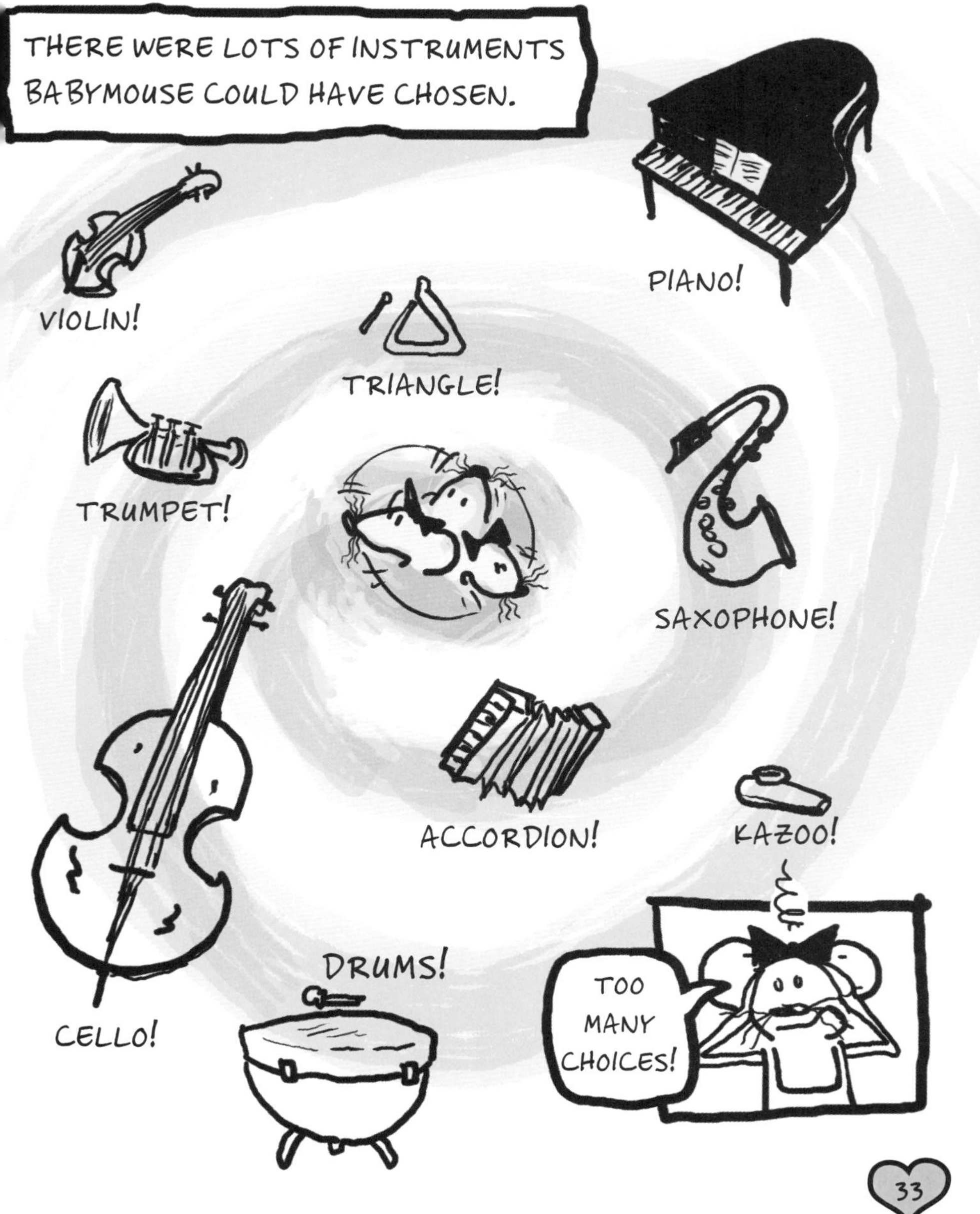
THERE WERE LOTS OF INSTRUMENTS BABYMOUSE COULD HAVE CHOSEN.
VIOLIN!
TRIANGLE!
PIANO!
TRUMPET!
SAXOPHONE!
ACCORDION!
KAZOO!
CELLO!
DRUMS!
TOO MANY CHOICES!

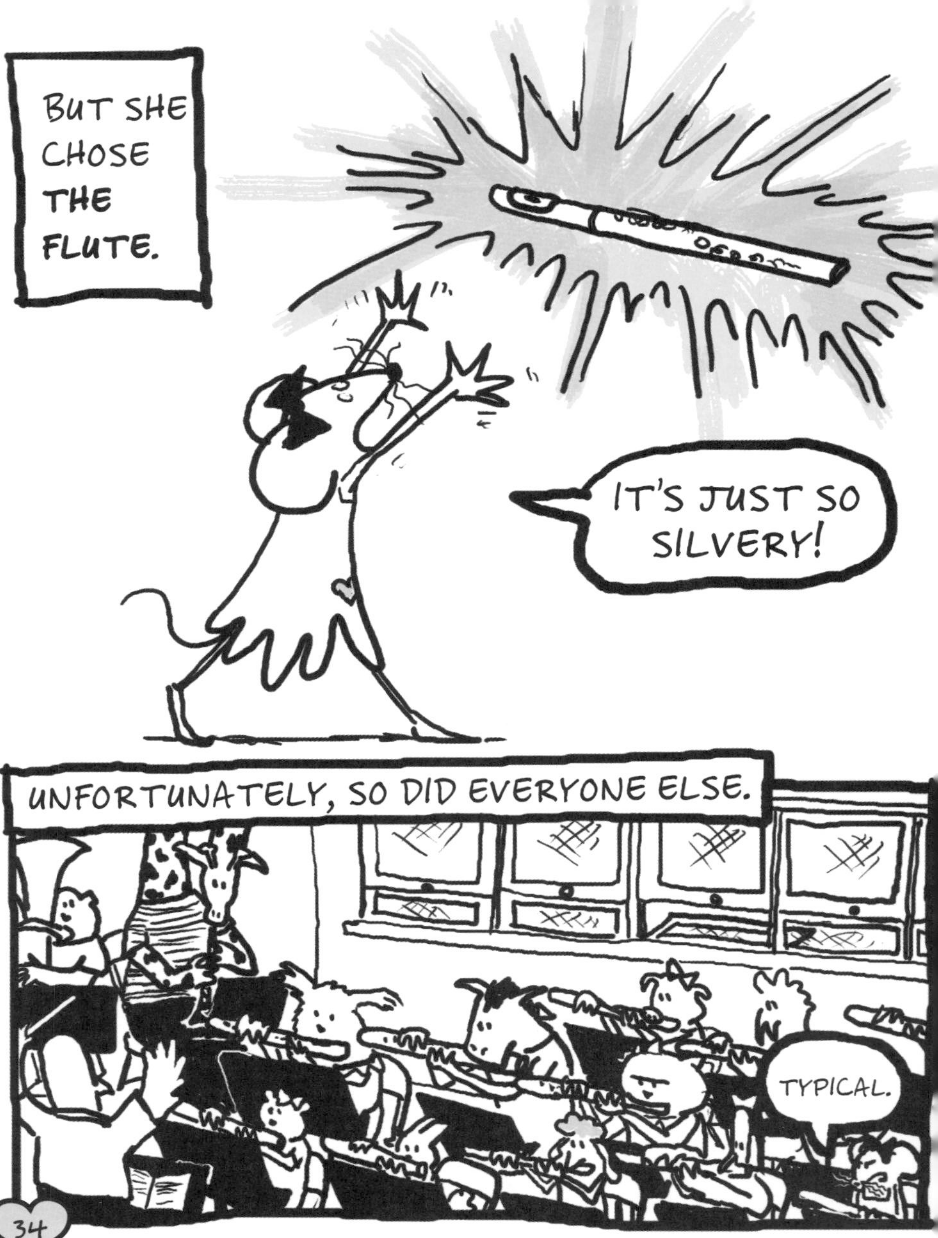
BUT SHE CHOSE **THE FLUTE.**
IT'S JUST SO SILVERY!
UNFORTUNATELY, SO DID EVERYONE ELSE.
TYPICAL.

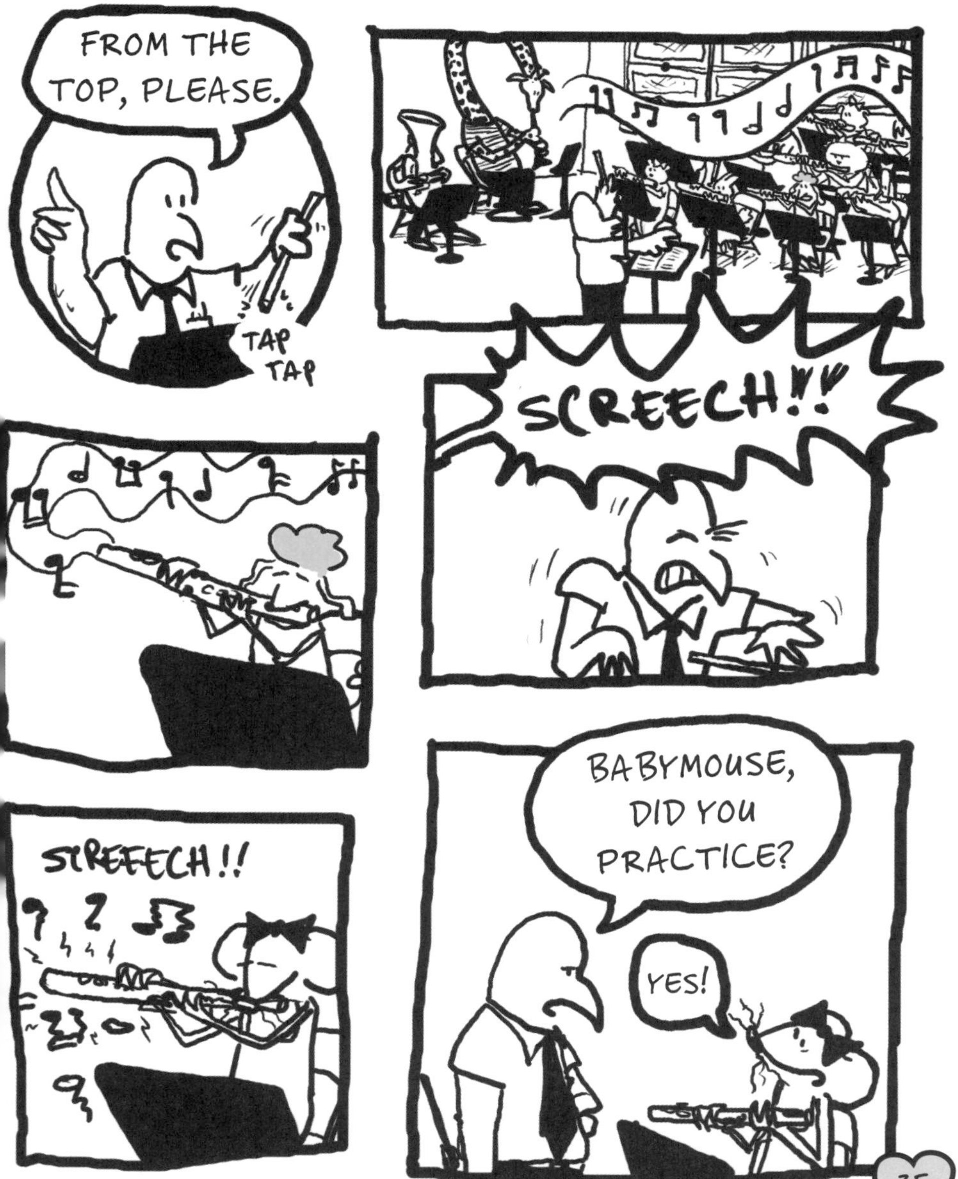
FROM THE TOP, PLEASE.
TAP TAP
SCREECH!!!
SCREEECH!!
BABYMOUSE, DID YOU PRACTICE?
YES!

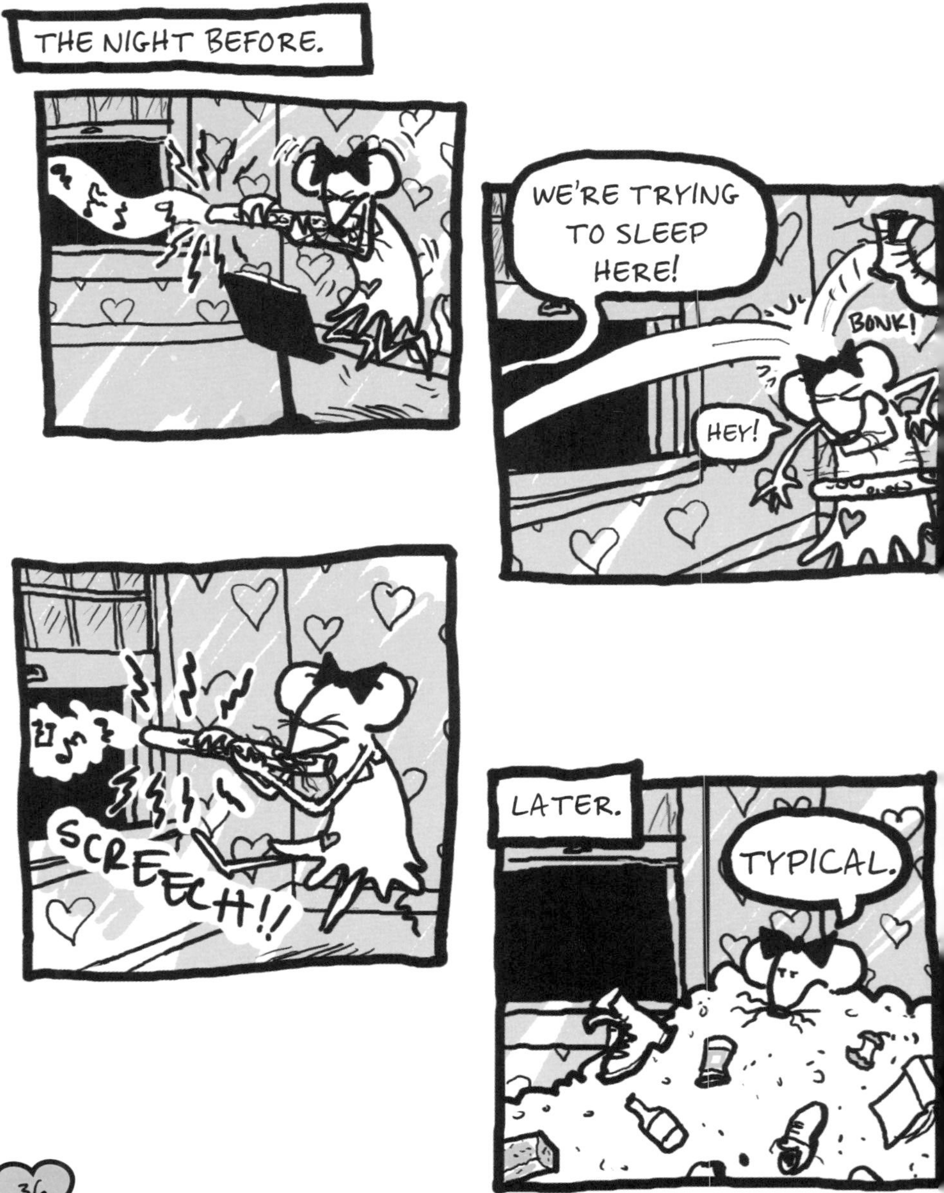
THE NIGHT BEFORE.
WE'RE TRYING TO SLEEP HERE!
BONK!
HEY!
SCREEECH!!
LATER.
TYPICAL.

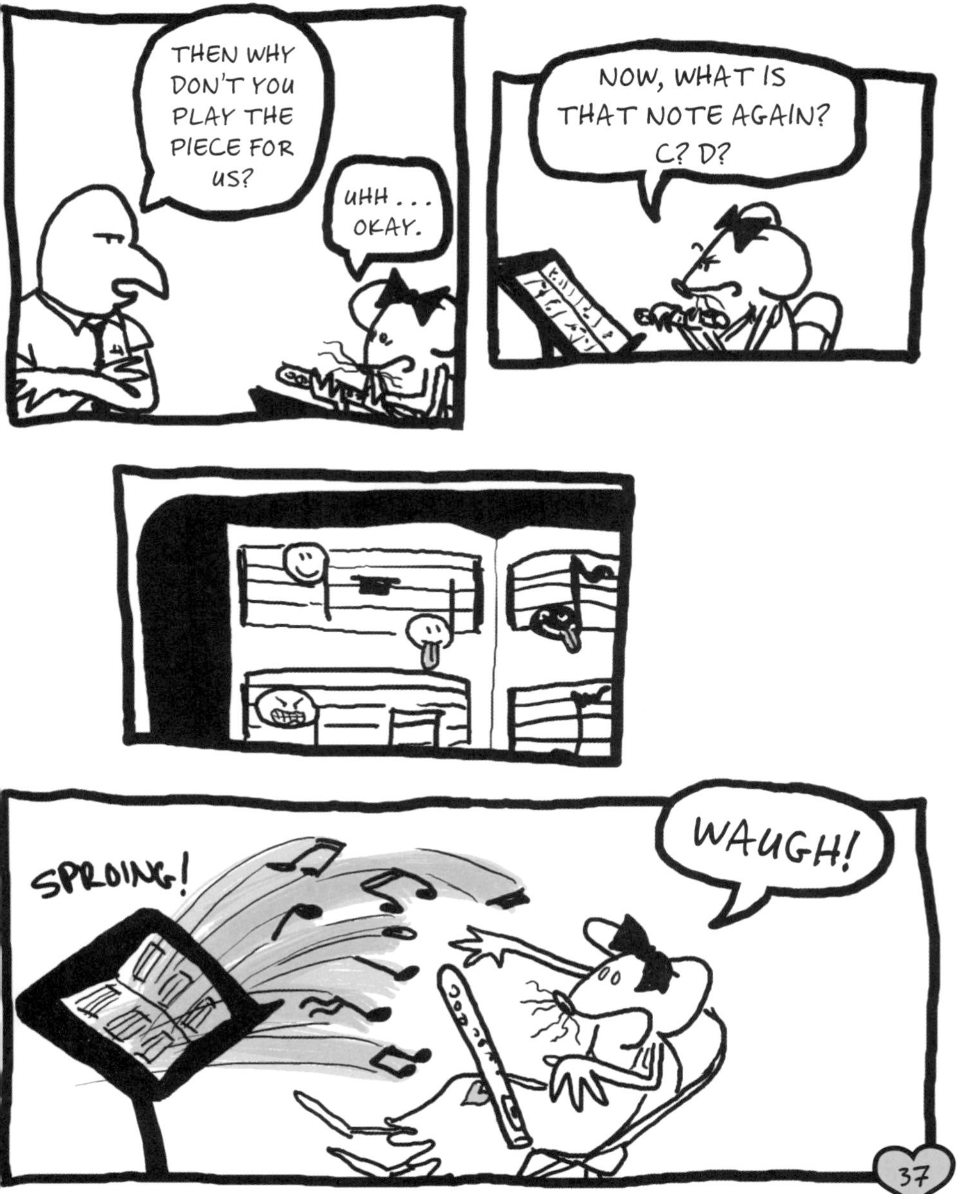
THEN WHY DON'T YOU PLAY THE PIECE FOR US?
UHH . . . OKAY.
NOW, WHAT IS THAT NOTE AGAIN? C? D?
SPROING!
WAUGH!

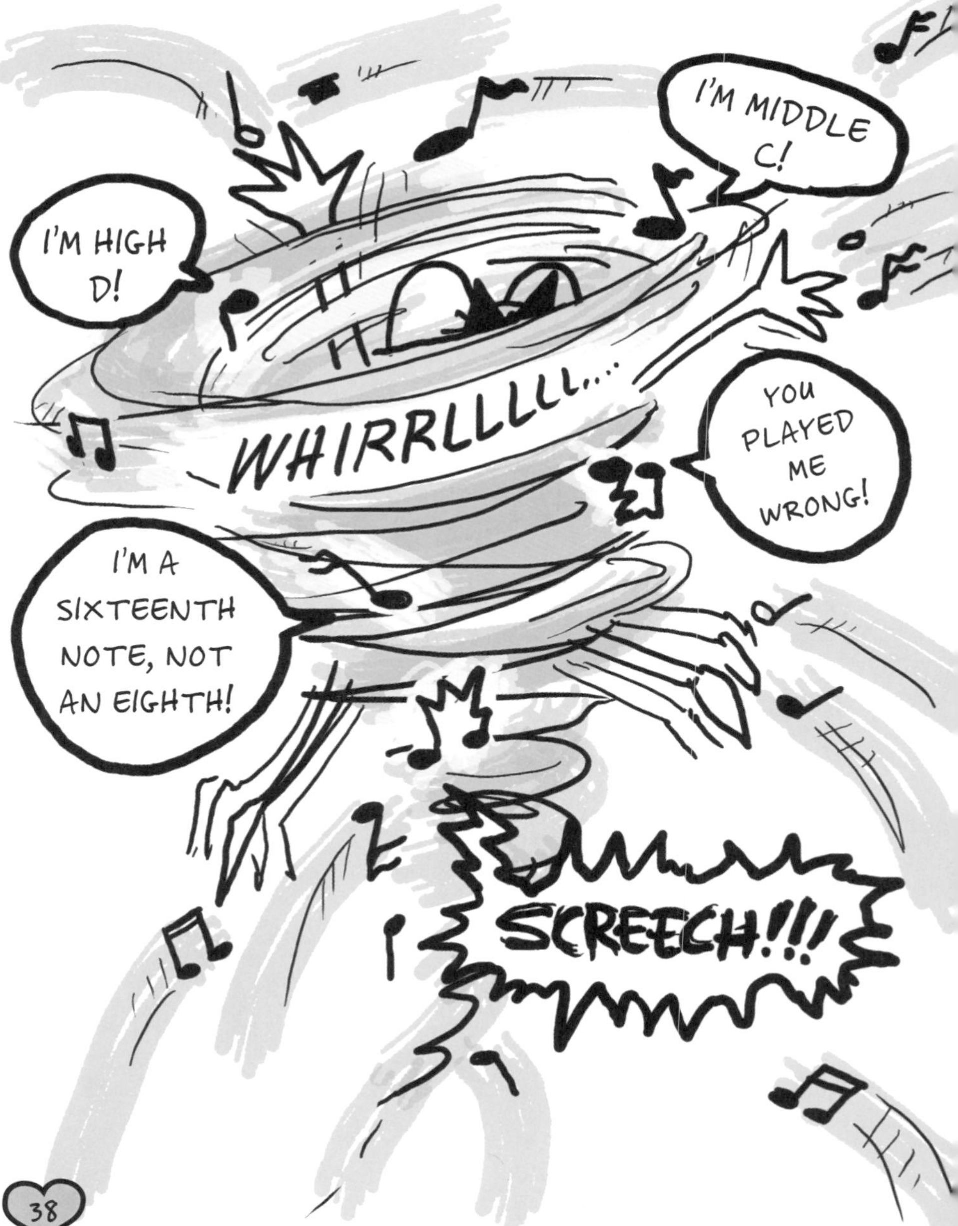
I'M MIDDLE C!
I'M HIGH D!
WHIRRLLLLL....
YOU PLAYED ME WRONG!
I'M A SIXTEENTH NOTE, NOT AN EIGHTH!
SCREECH!!!

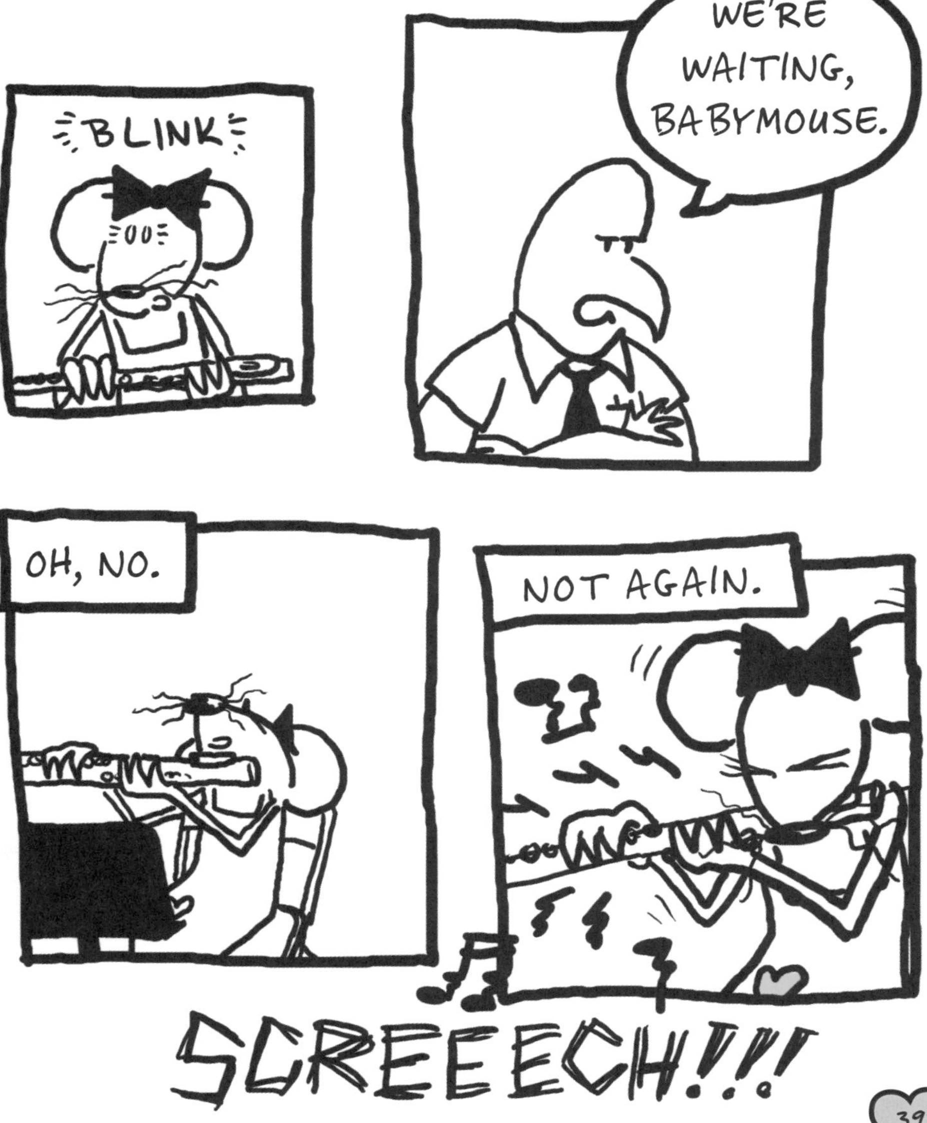
BLINK
WE'RE WAITING, BABYMOUSE.
OH, NO.
NOT AGAIN.
SCREEECH!!!!

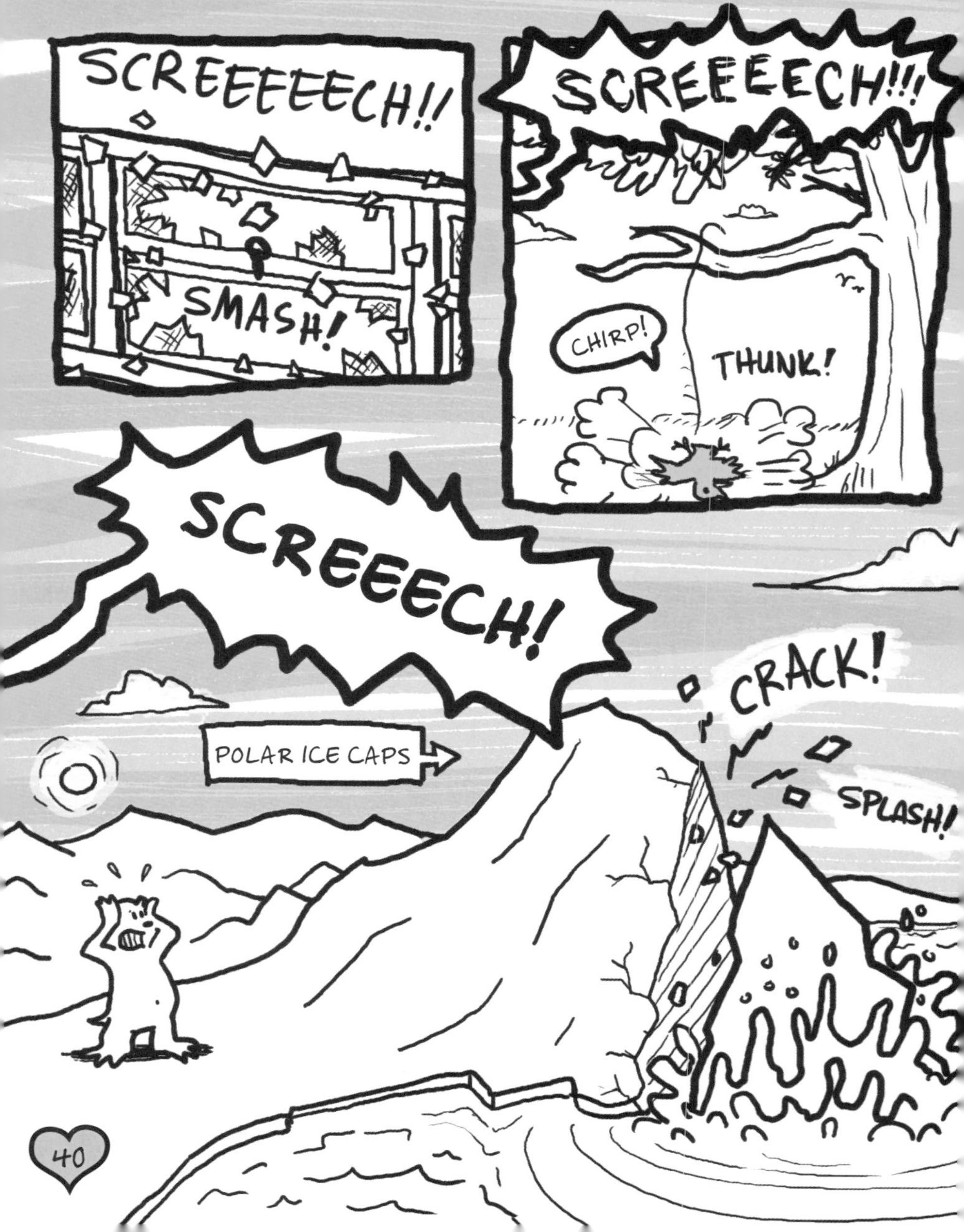
SCREEEEEECH!!
SMASH!
SCREEEEECH!!!
CHIRP!
THUNK!
SCREEEECH!
POLAR ICE CAPS
CRACK!
SPLASH!

YES, BABYMOUSE LOVED PLAYING THE FLUTE. SHE JUST WASN'T VERY GOOD AT IT.

AFTER CLASS.

BABYMOUSE REMEMBERED THE LAST CONCERT.

BABYMOUSE! BABYMOUSE!

IS BABYMOUSE UP THERE?

YES, GRAMPAMOUSE.

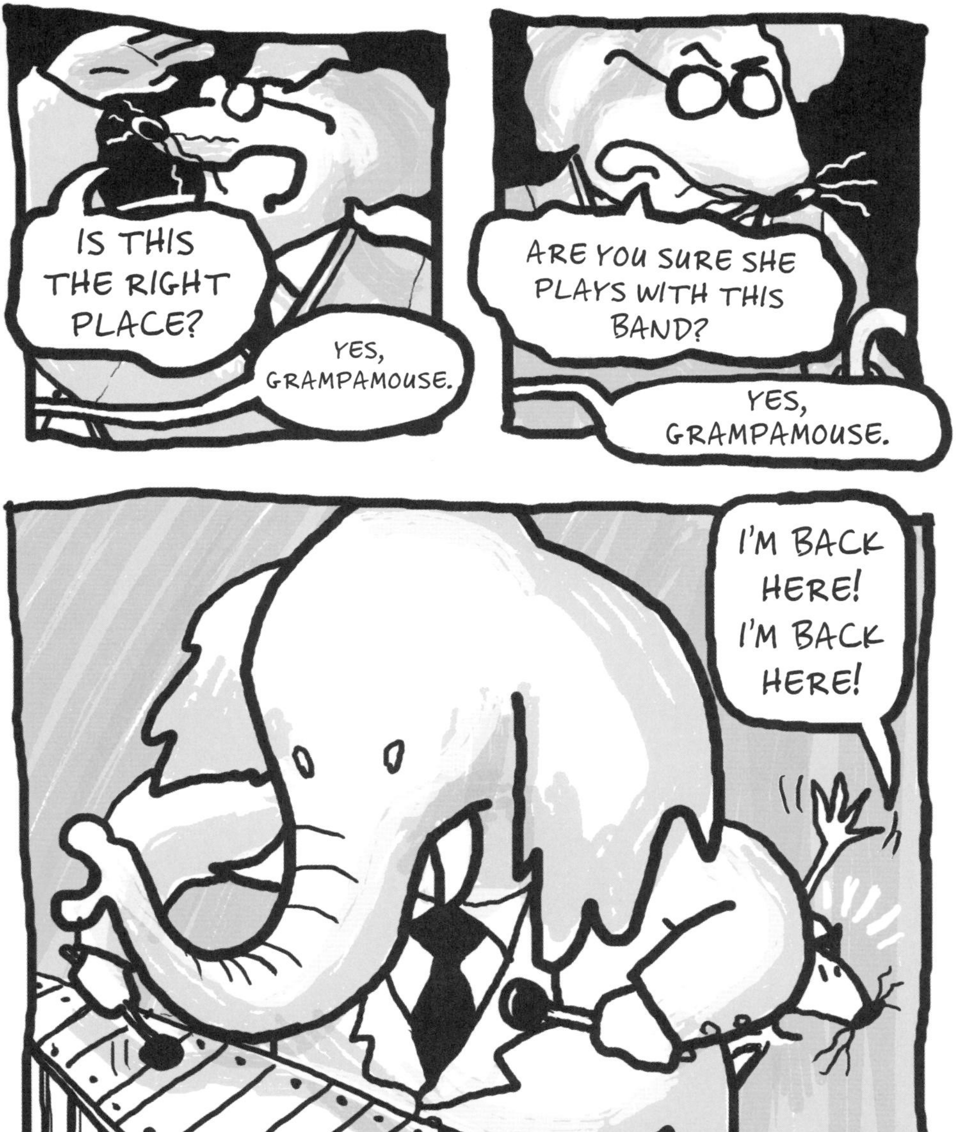
IS THIS THE RIGHT PLACE?
YES, GRAMPAMOUSE.
ARE YOU SURE SHE PLAYS WITH THIS BAND?
YES, GRAMPAMOUSE.
I'M BACK HERE! I'M BACK HERE!

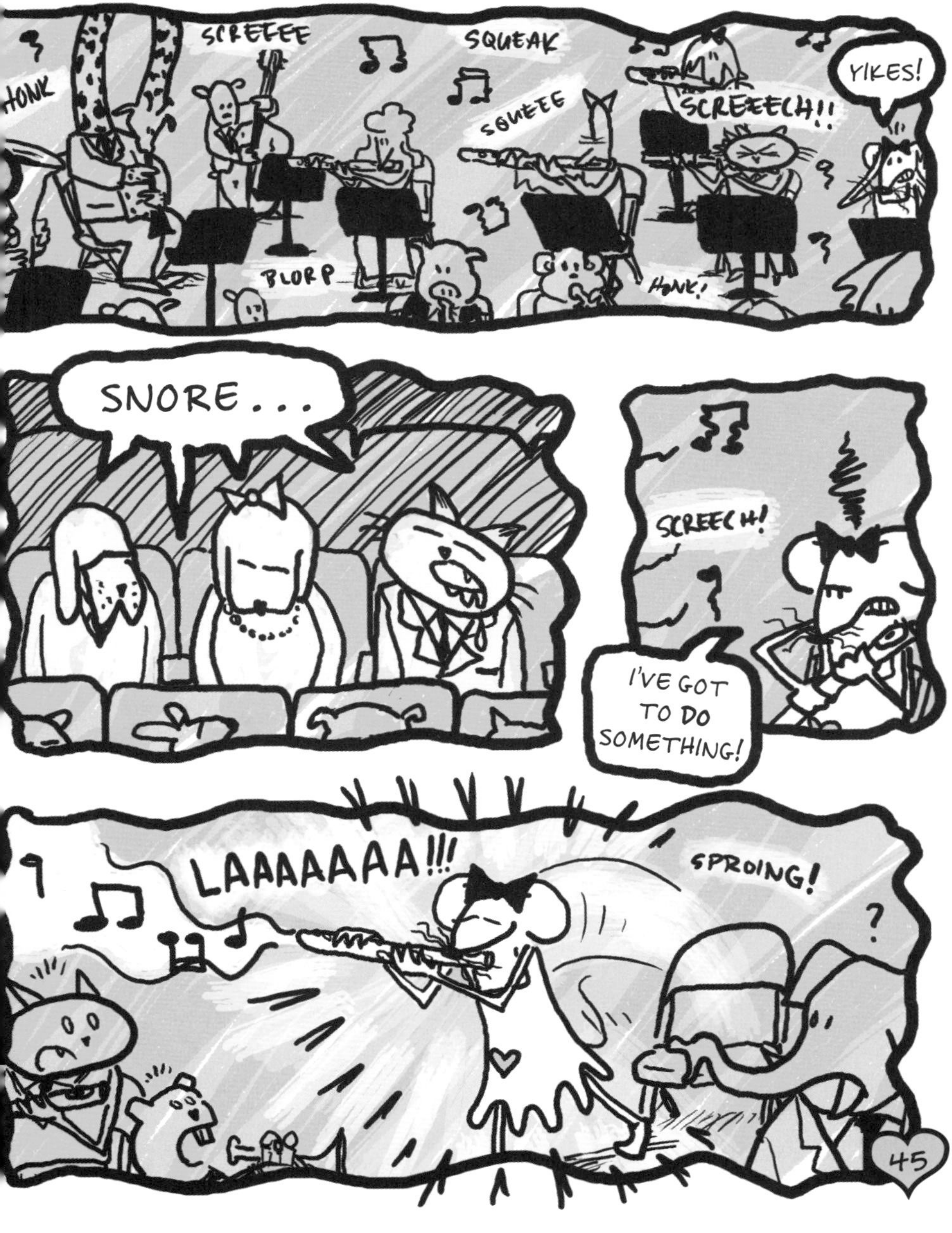
HONK
SCREEEE
SQUEAK
SQUEEE
SCREEEECH!!
YIKES!
BLORP
HONK!
SNORE...
SCREECH!
I'VE GOT TO DO SOMETHING!
LAAAAAAA!!!
SPROING!
?

BABYMOUSE!

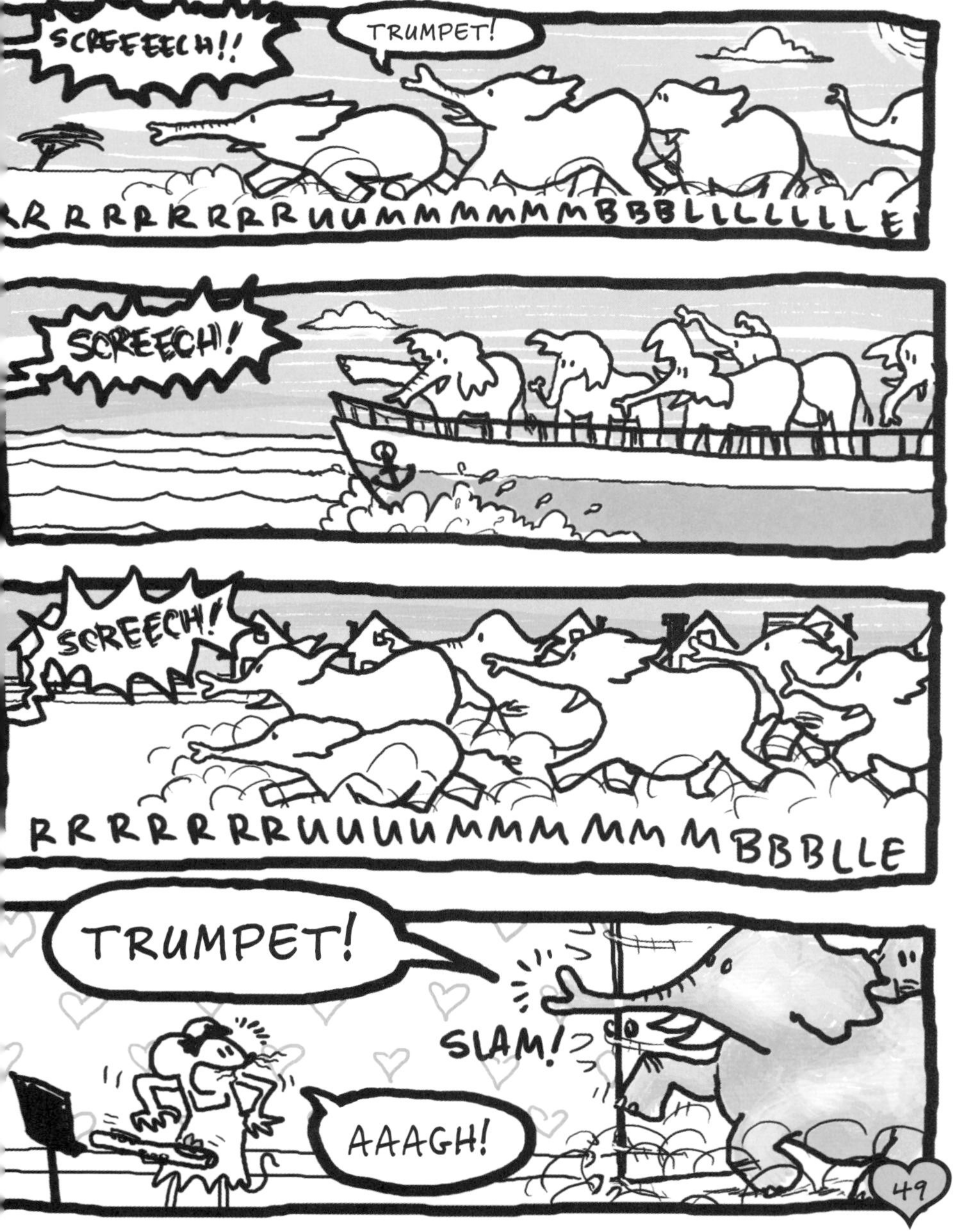
SCREEEECH!!
TRUMPET!
RRRRRRRRRUUMMMMMMMBBBLLLLLLLLE
SCREECH!
SCREECH!
RRRRRRRRUUUUUMMMMMMMBBBLLE
TRUMPET!
SLAM!
AAAGH!

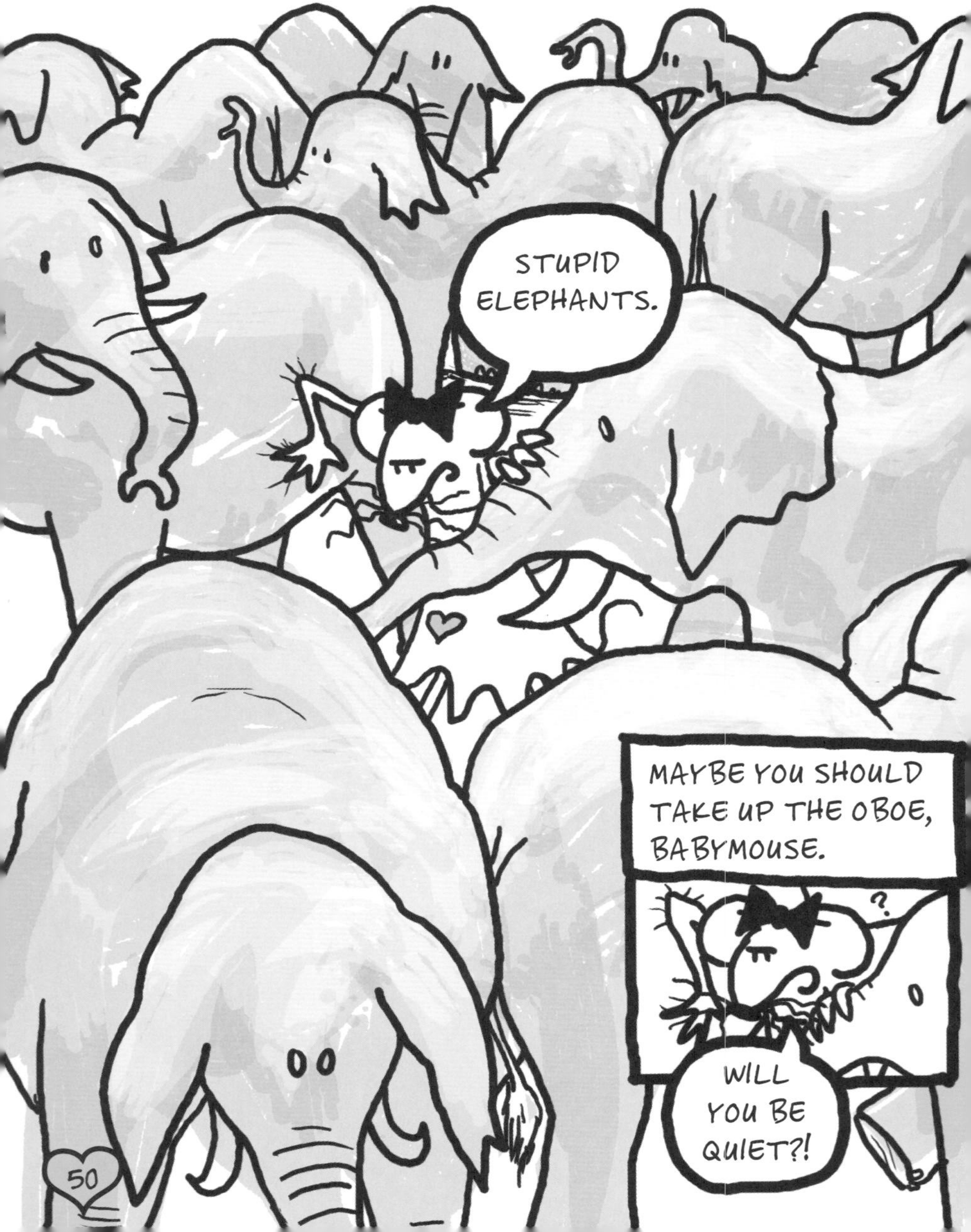
STUPID ELEPHANTS.
MAYBE YOU SHOULD TAKE UP THE OBOE, BABYMOUSE.
WILL YOU BE QUIET?!

53

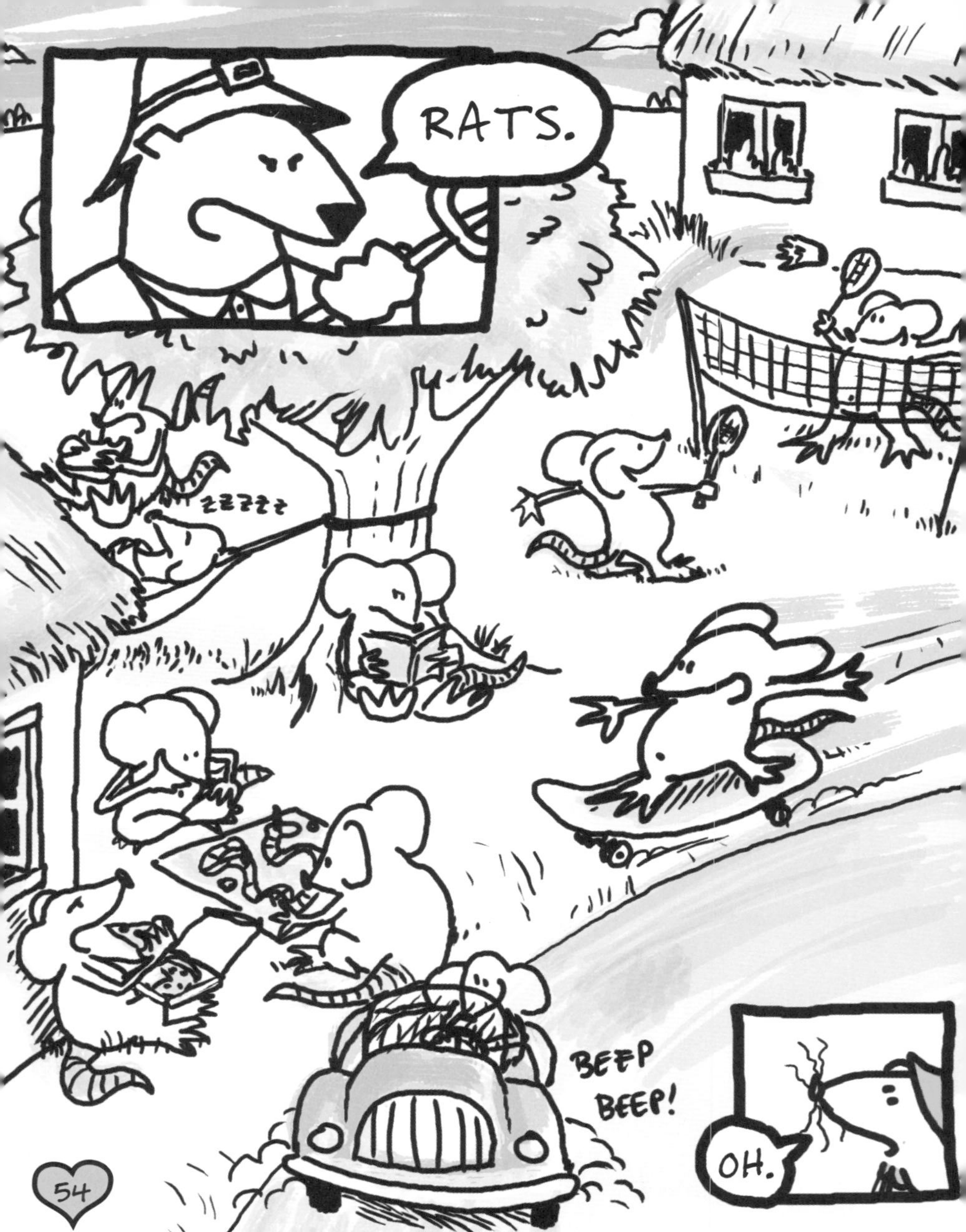
RATS.
zzzzzz
BEEP BEEP!
OH.

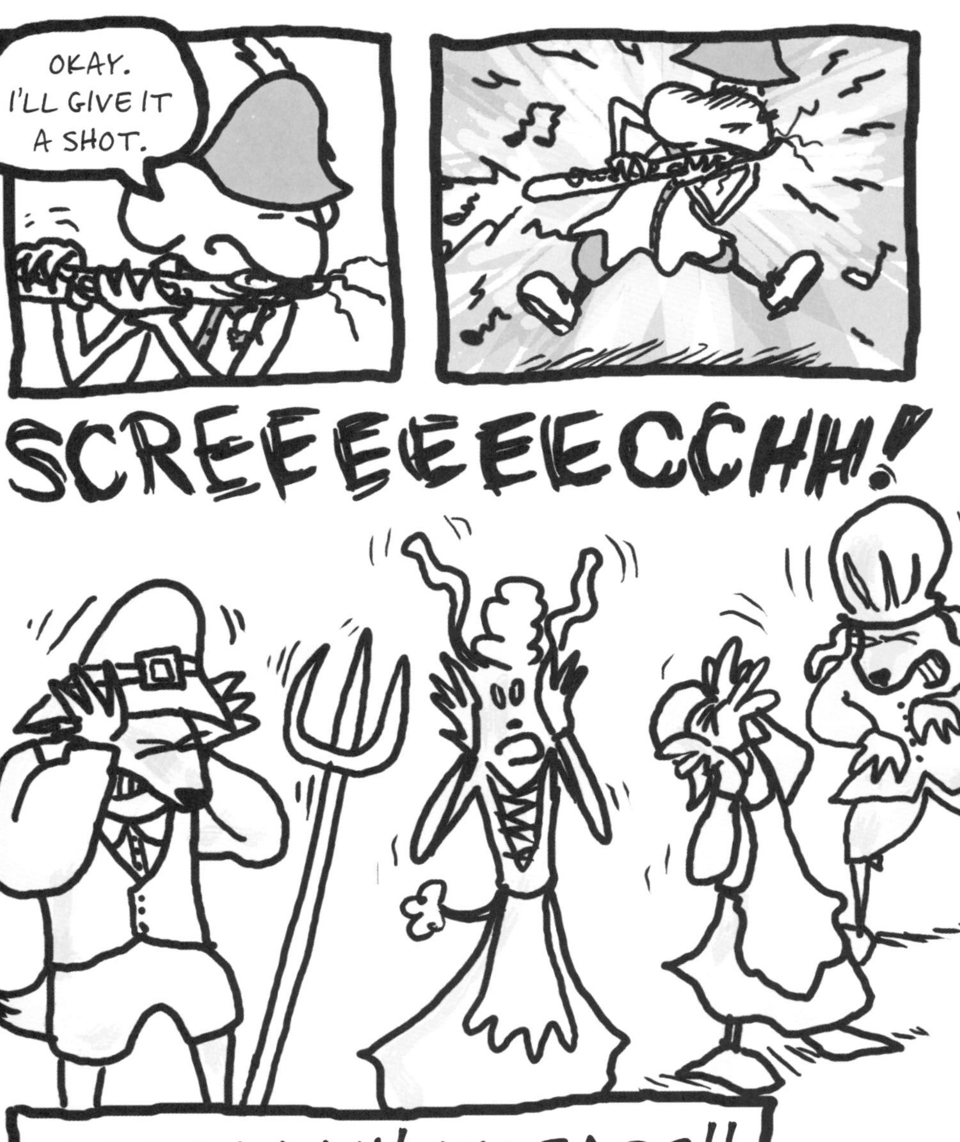
OKAY. I'LL GIVE IT A SHOT.
SCREEEEEEECCHH!
AAAAAAAH! MY EARS!!

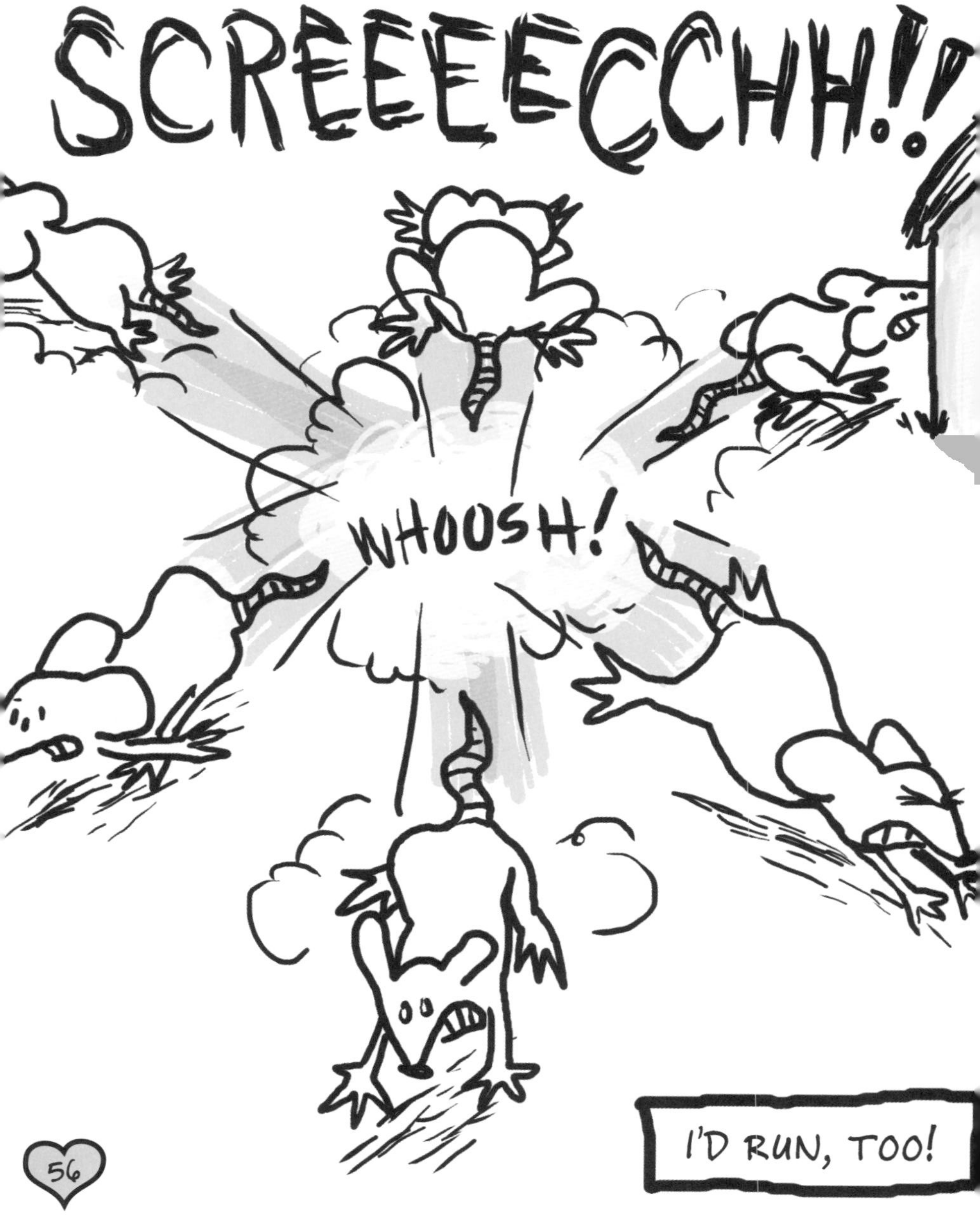
SCREEEECCHH!!
WHOOSH!
I'D RUN, TOO!

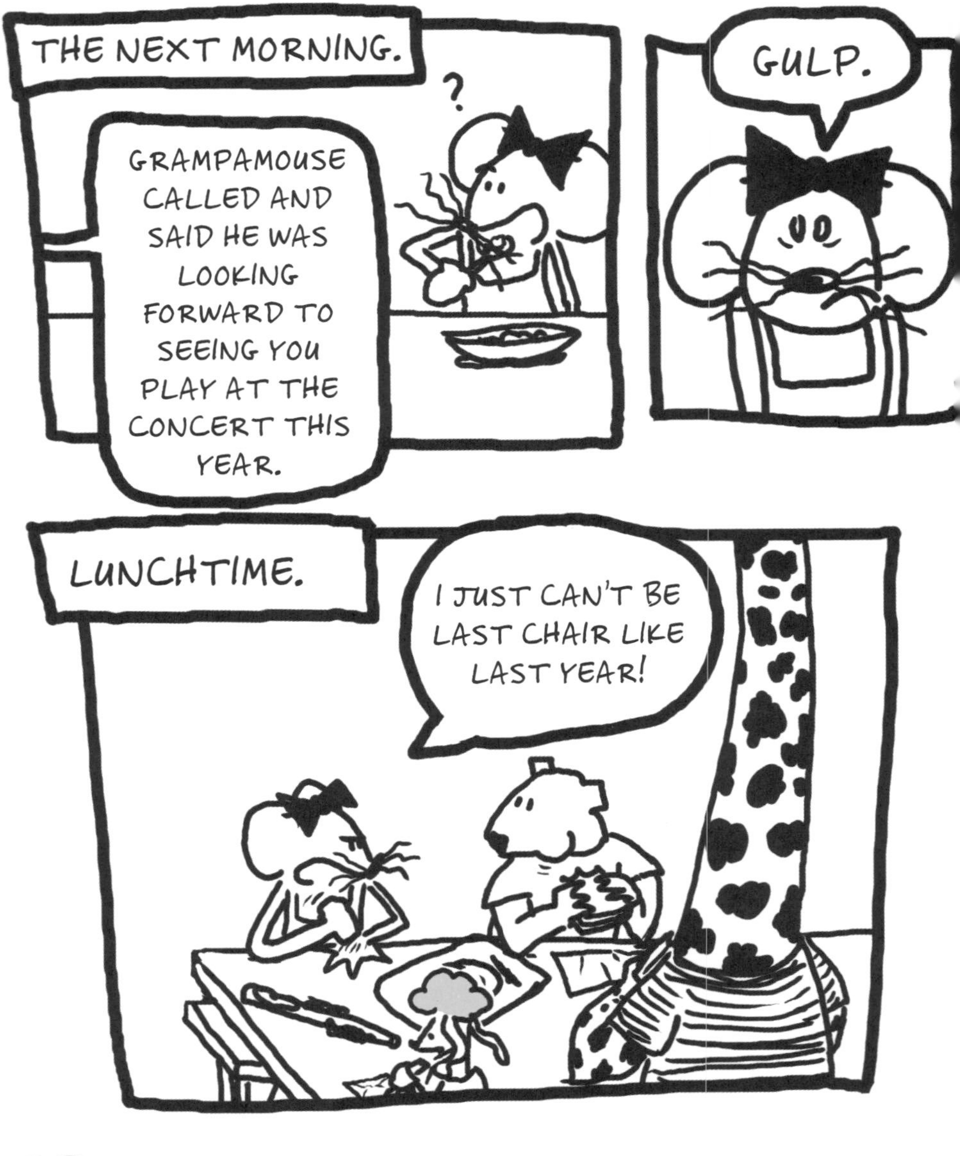
THE NEXT MORNING.
GRAMPAMOUSE CALLED AND SAID HE WAS LOOKING FORWARD TO SEEING YOU PLAY AT THE CONCERT THIS YEAR.
?
GULP.
LUNCHTIME.
I JUST CAN'T BE LAST CHAIR LIKE LAST YEAR!

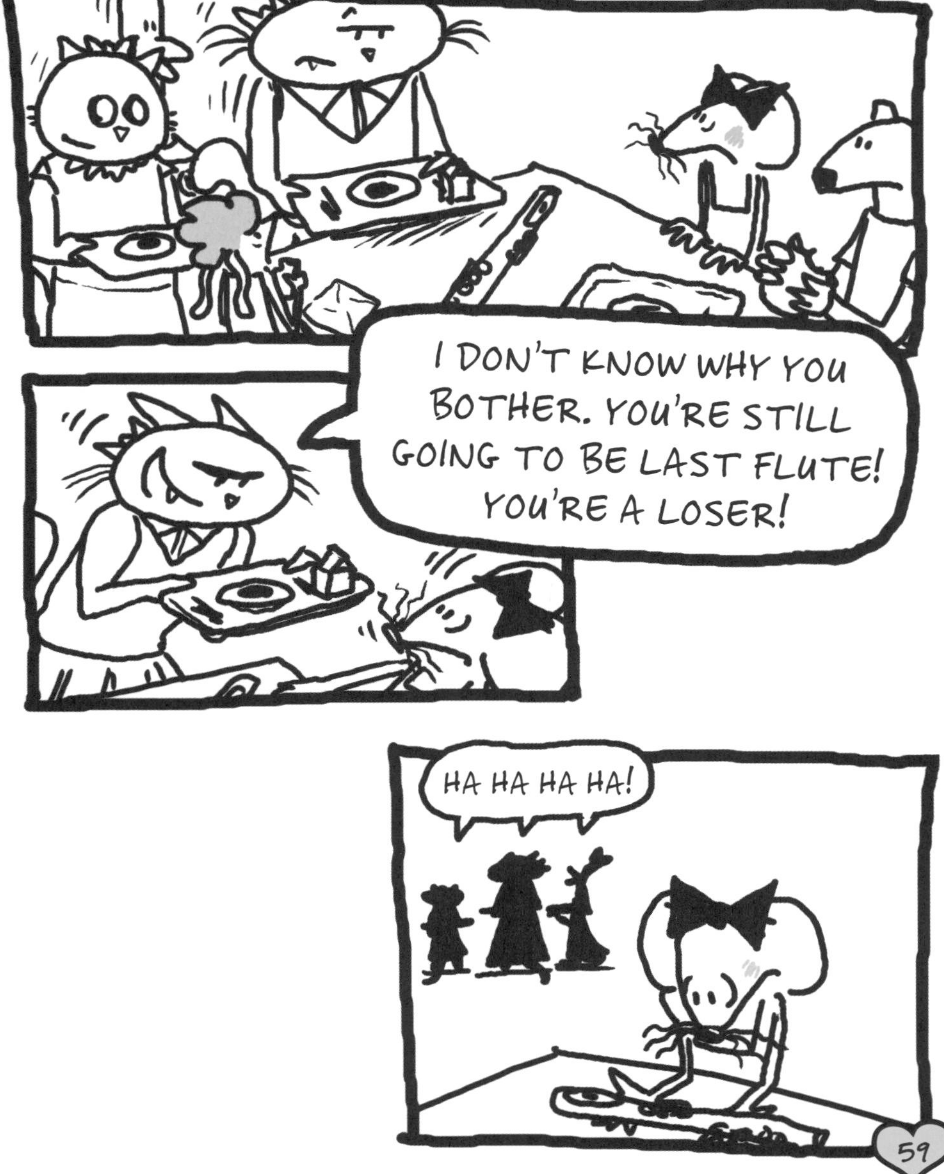
I DON'T KNOW WHY YOU BOTHER. YOU'RE STILL GOING TO BE LAST FLUTE! YOU'RE A LOSER!
HA HA HA HA!

I'LL HELP YOU, BABYMOUSE.
YOU WILL? WHY?
I HAVE MY REASONS.
PAT PAT
COME TO MY HOUSE AFTER SCHOOL.

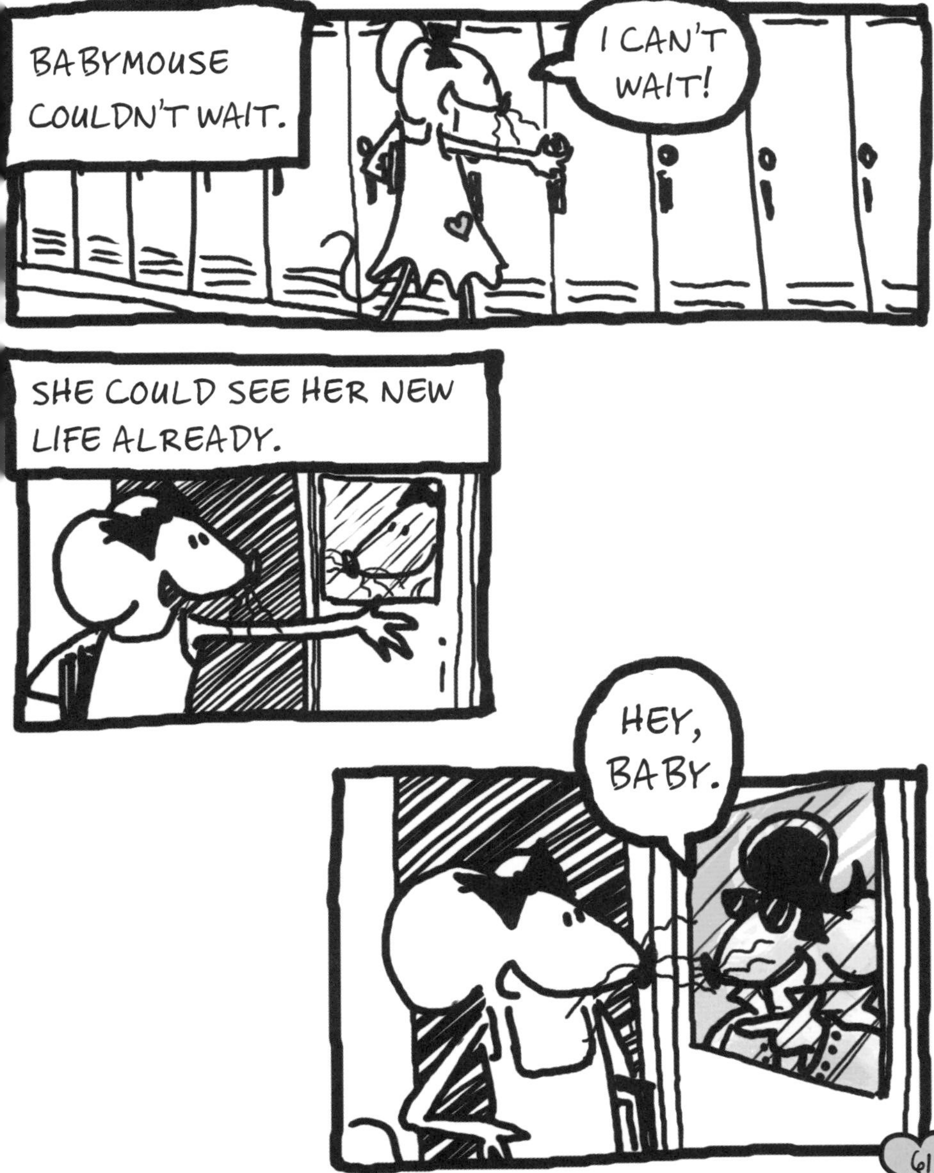
BABYMOUSE COULDN'T WAIT.
I CAN'T WAIT!
SHE COULD SEE HER NEW LIFE ALREADY.
HEY, BABY.

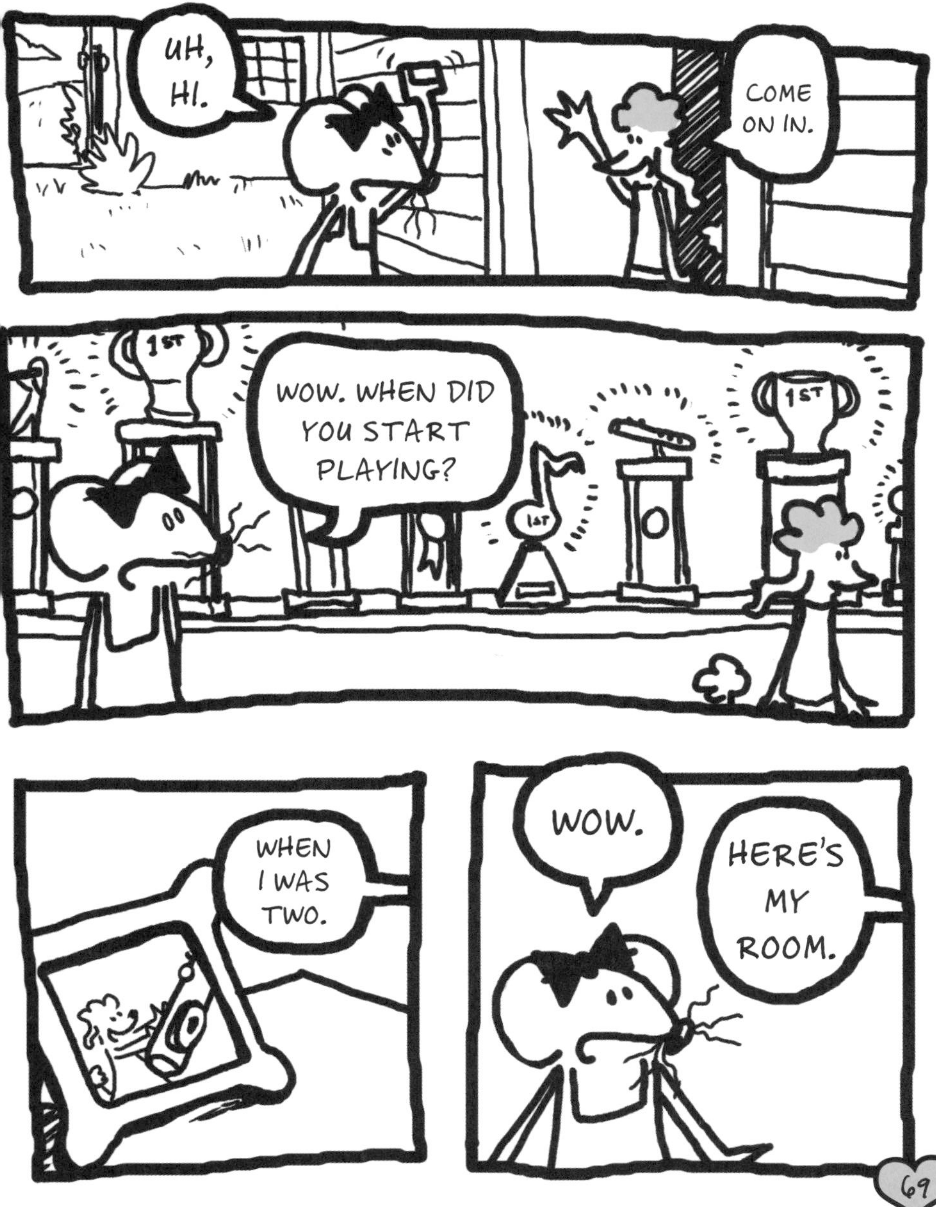
UH, HI.
COME ON IN.
WOW. WHEN DID YOU START PLAYING?
1ST
1ST
1ST
WHEN I WAS TWO.
WOW.
HERE'S MY ROOM.

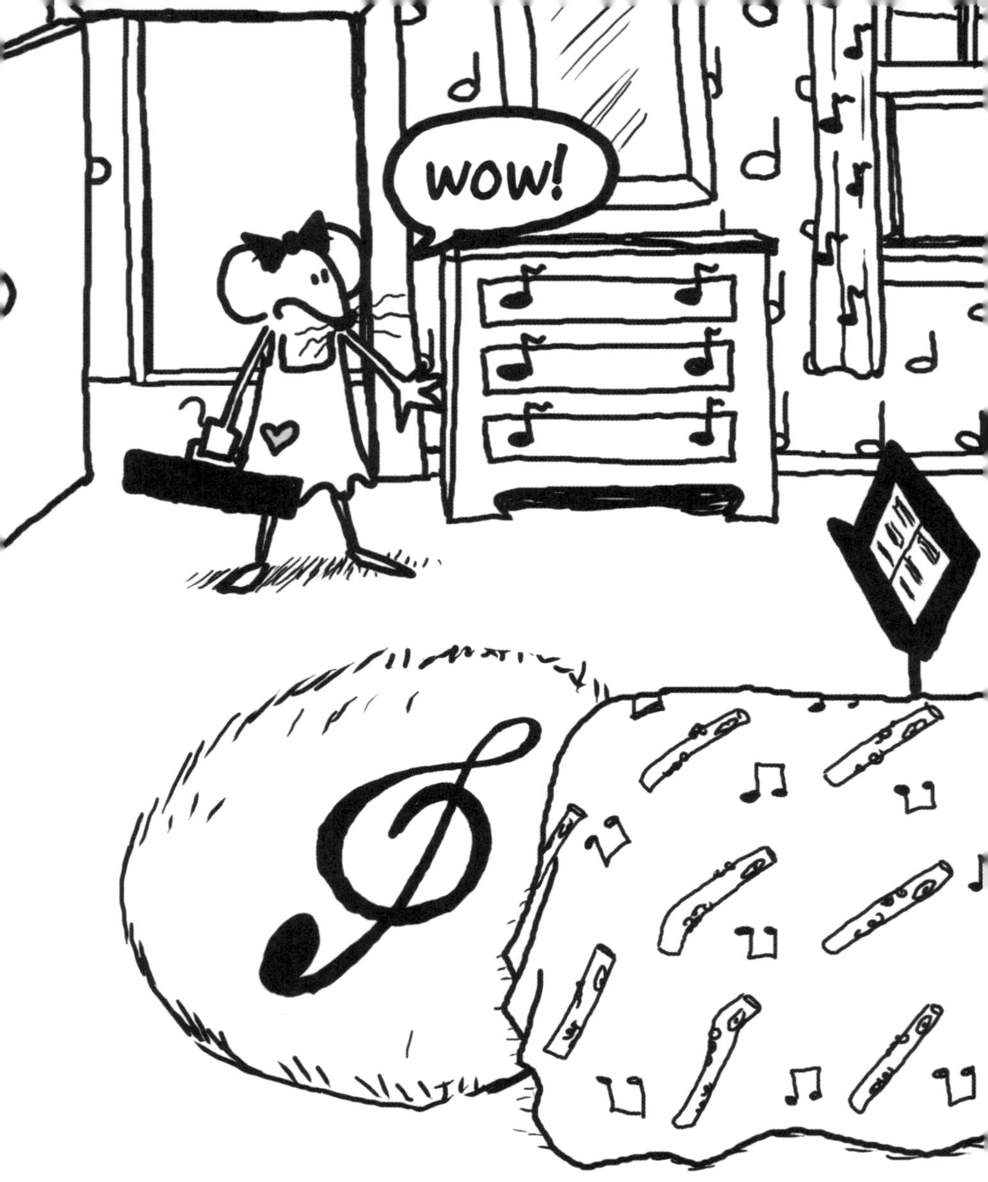
WOW!

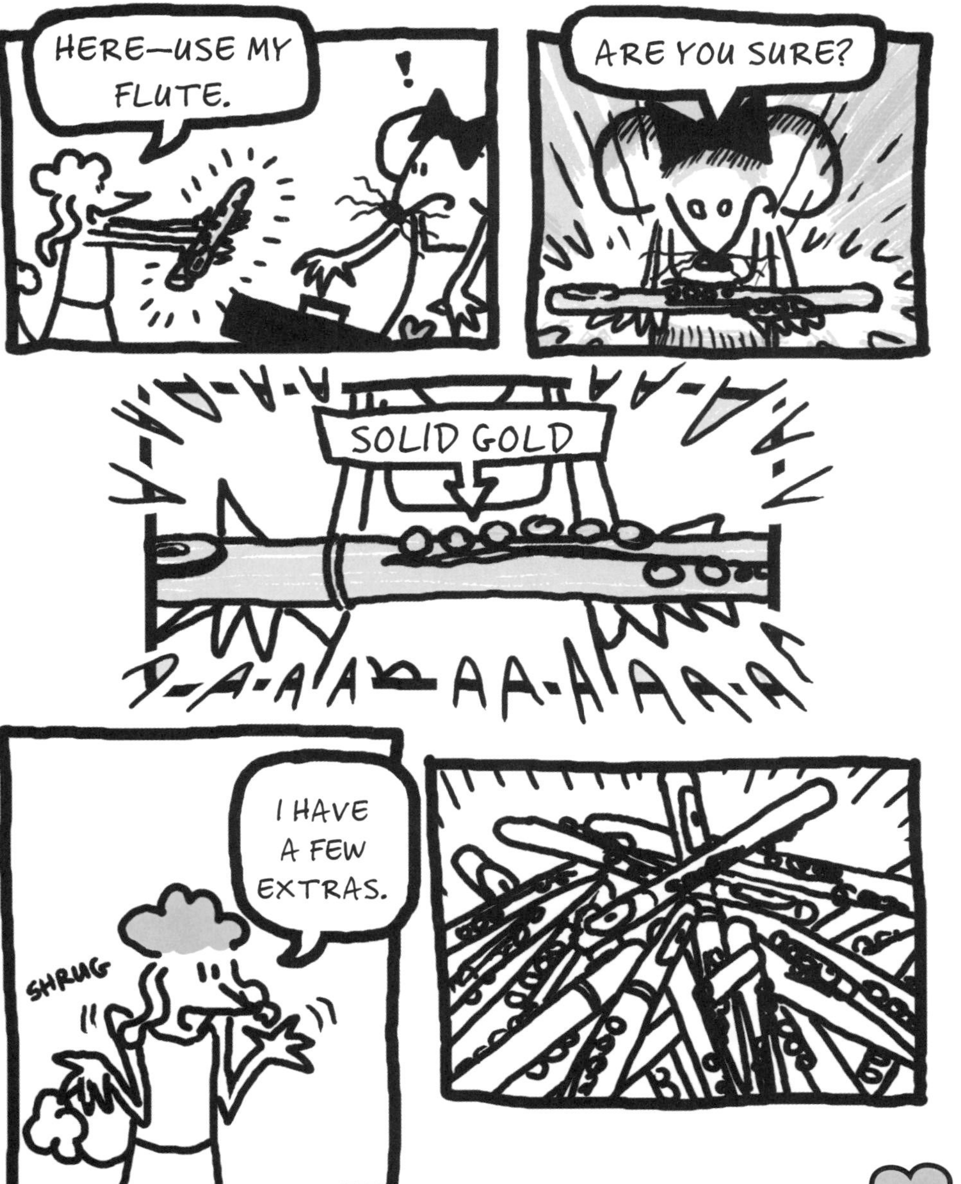
HERE—USE MY FLUTE.
!
ARE YOU SURE?
SOLID GOLD
SHRUG
I HAVE A FEW EXTRAS.

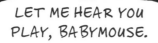

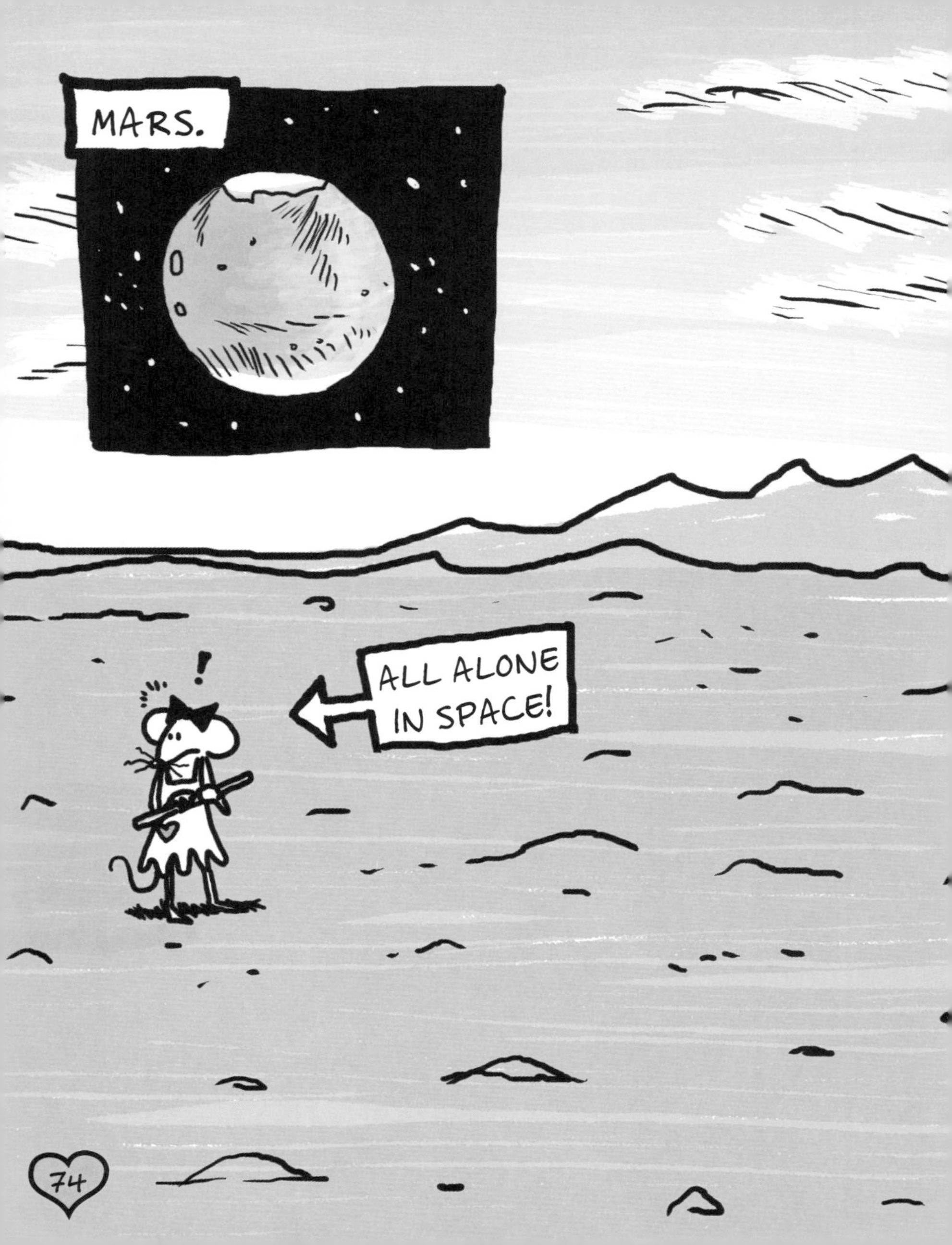
MARS.
!
ALL ALONE IN SPACE!

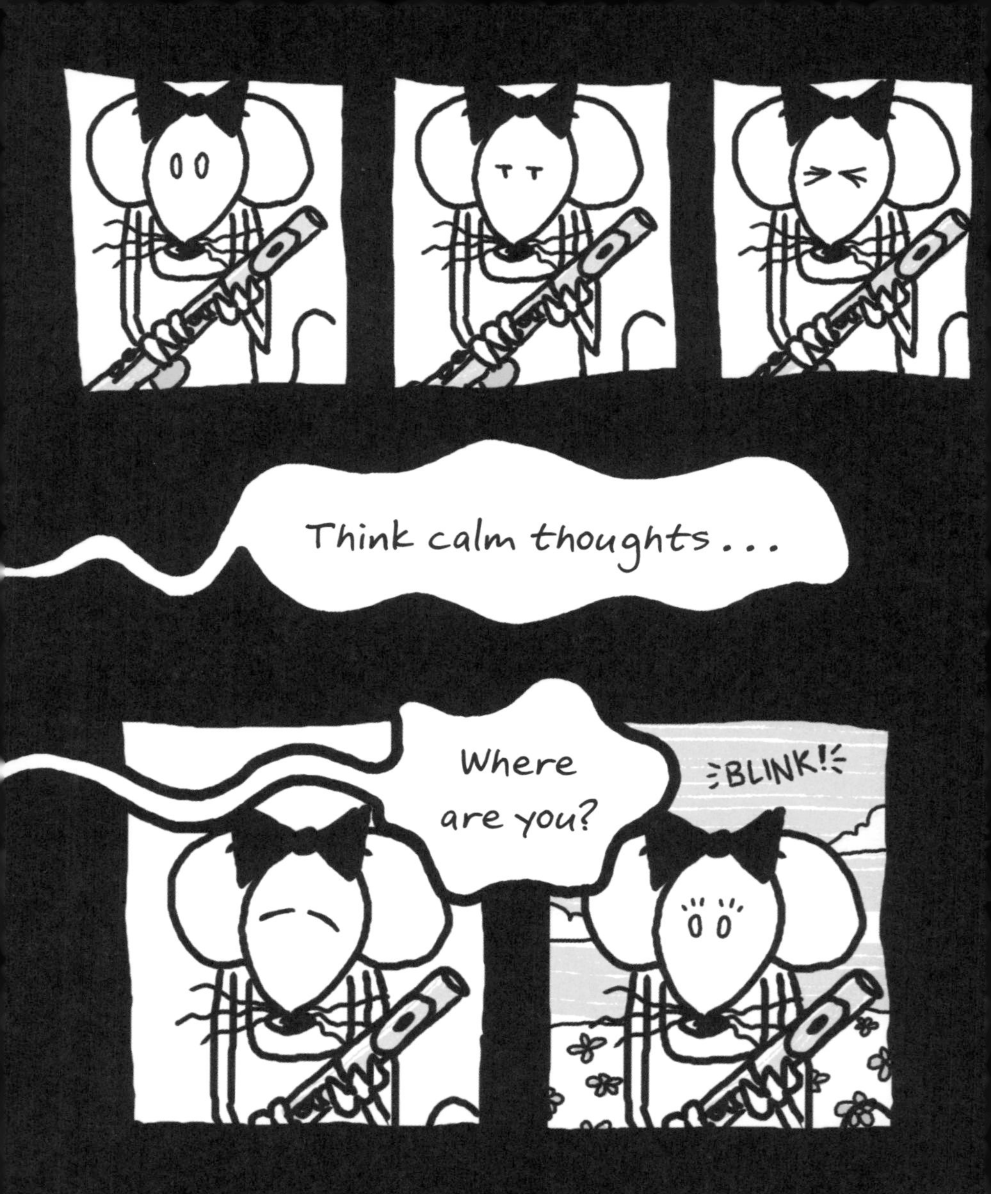

Think calm thoughts...
Where are you?
BLINK!

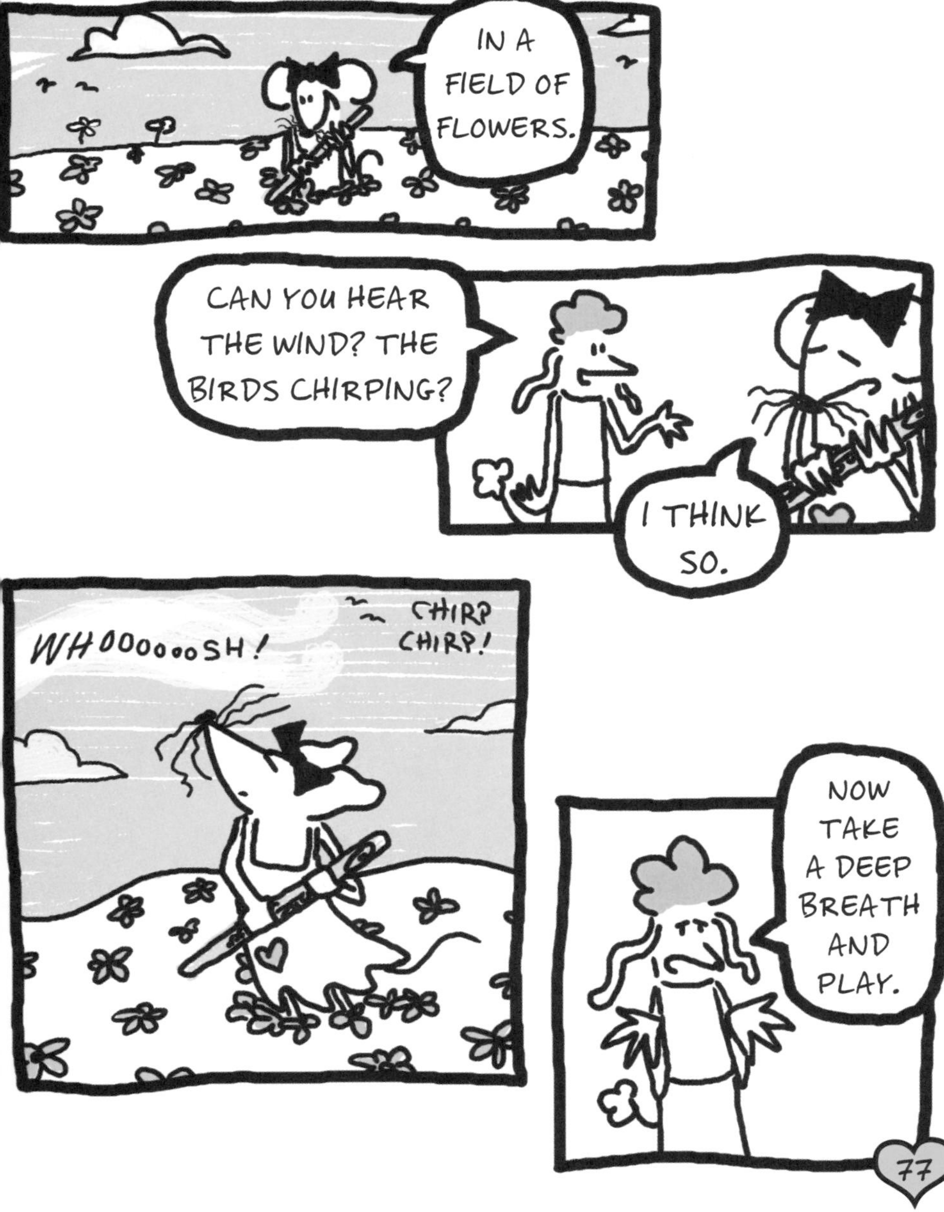
IN A FIELD OF FLOWERS.
CAN YOU HEAR THE WIND? THE BIRDS CHIRPING?
I THINK SO.
WHOOOOOOOSH!
CHIRP CHIRP!
NOW TAKE A DEEP BREATH AND PLAY.

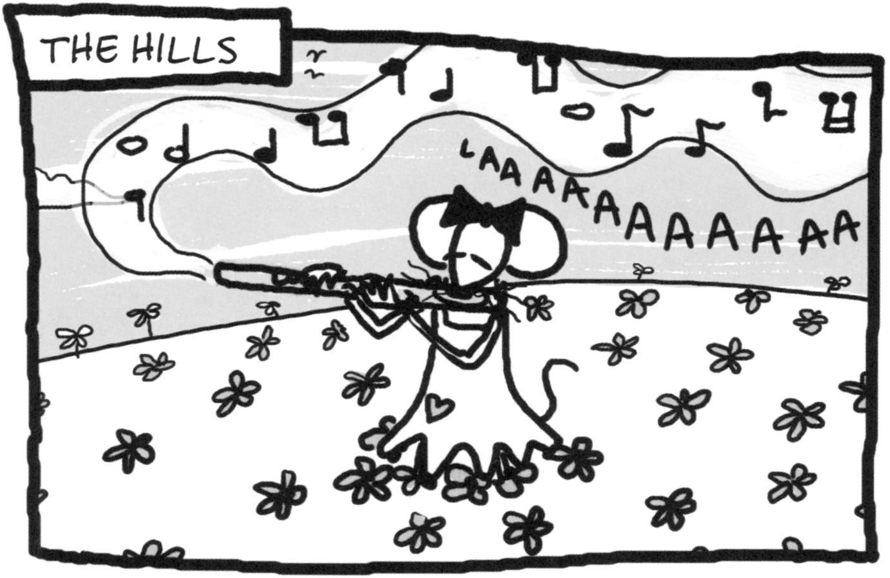
THE HILLS
LAAAAAAAAAAAAA

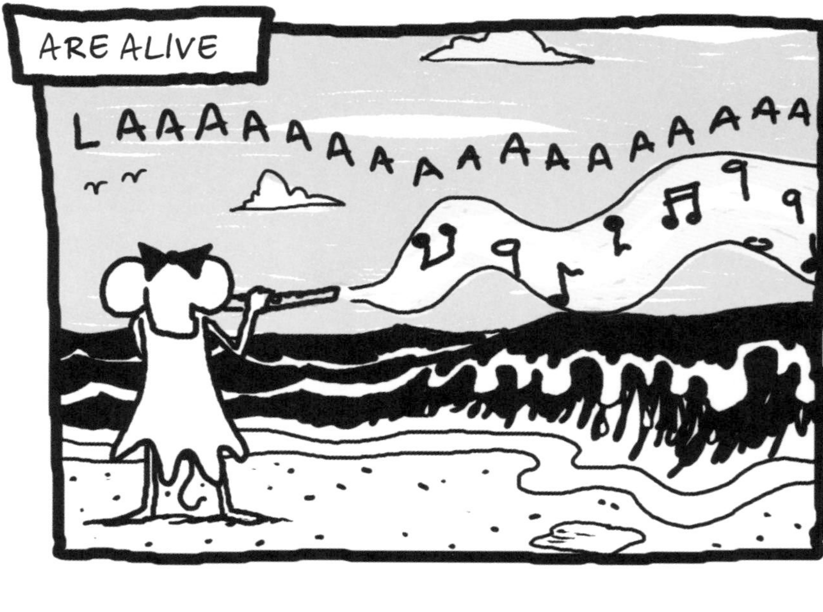
ARE ALIVE
LAAAAAAAAAAAAAAAAAAAAA

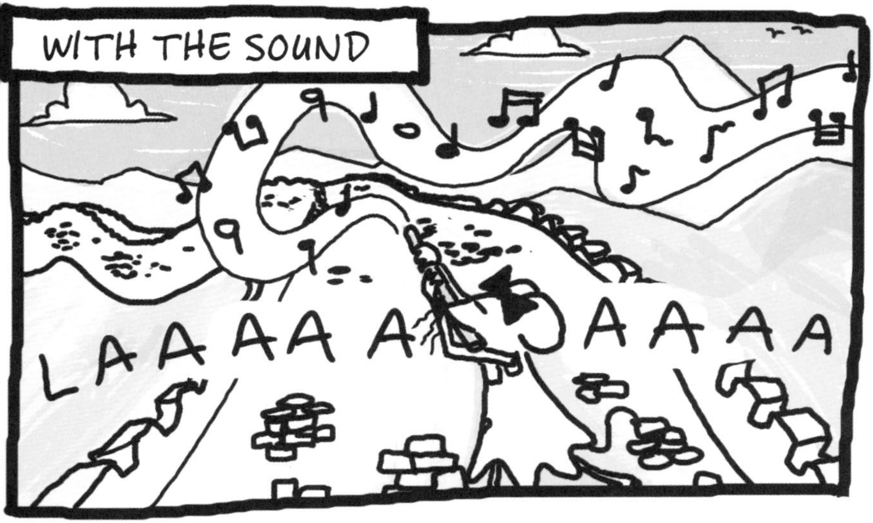
WITH THE SOUND
LAAAAA AAAAA

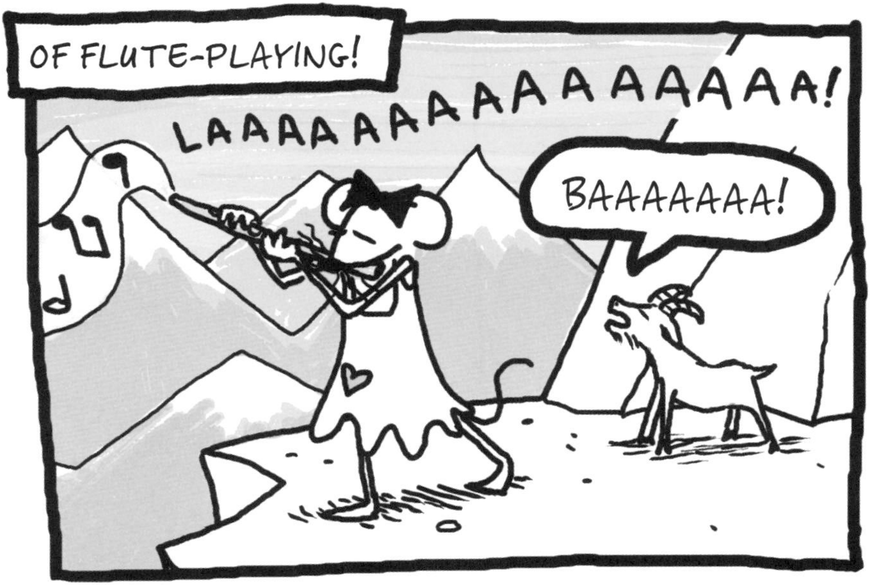
OF FLUTE-PLAYING!
LAAAAAAAAAAAAAAA!
BAAAAAAA!

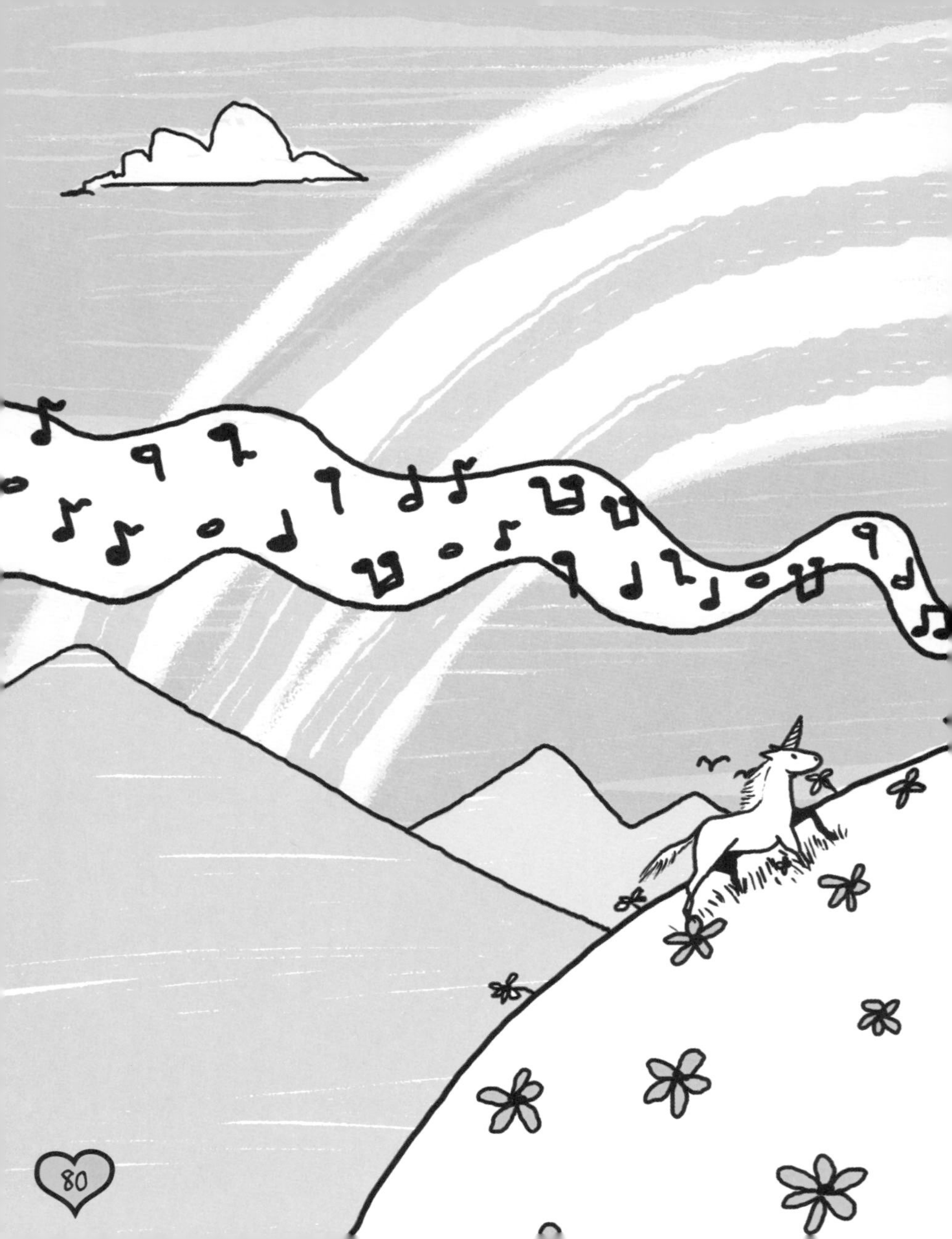

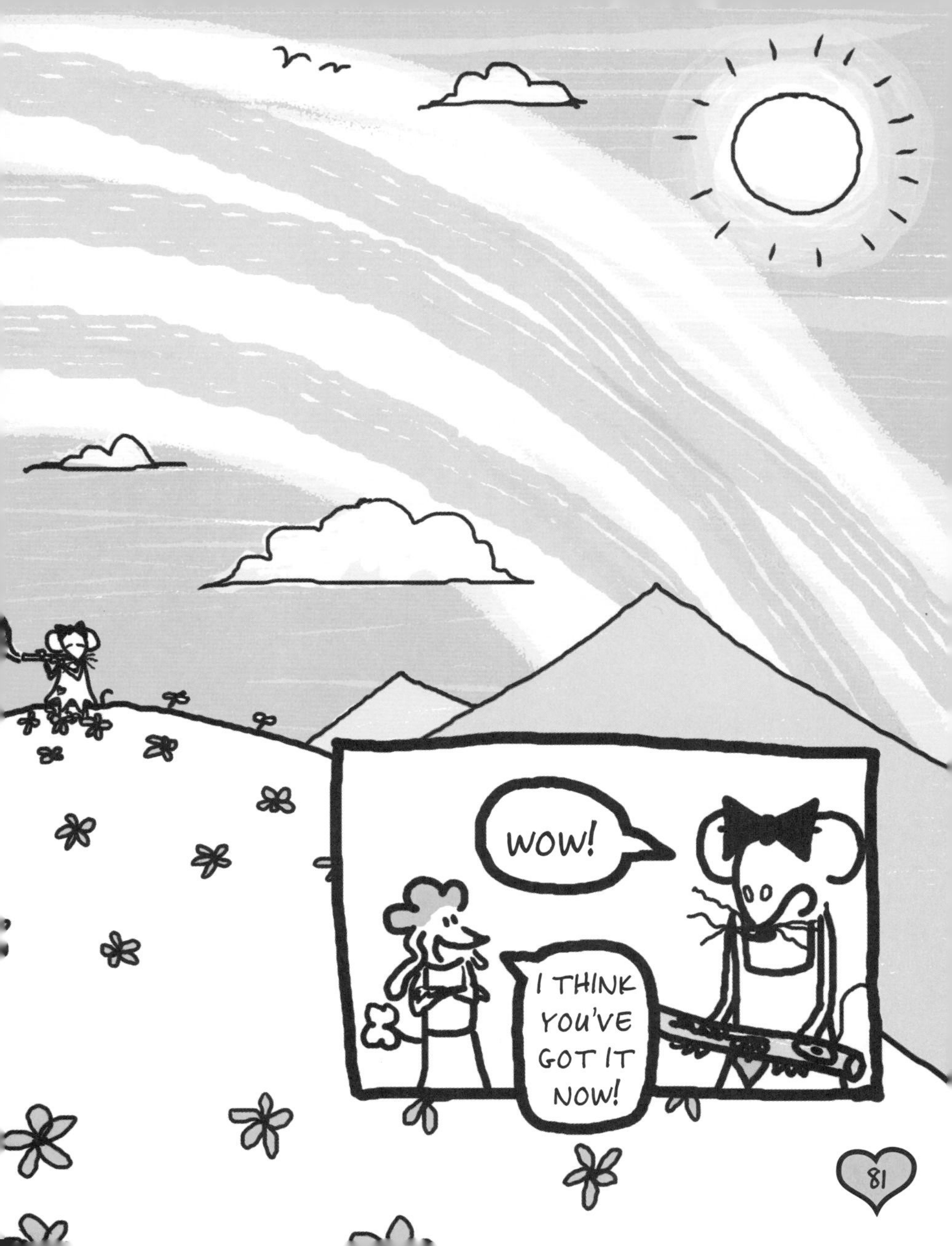
WOW!
I THINK YOU'VE GOT IT NOW!

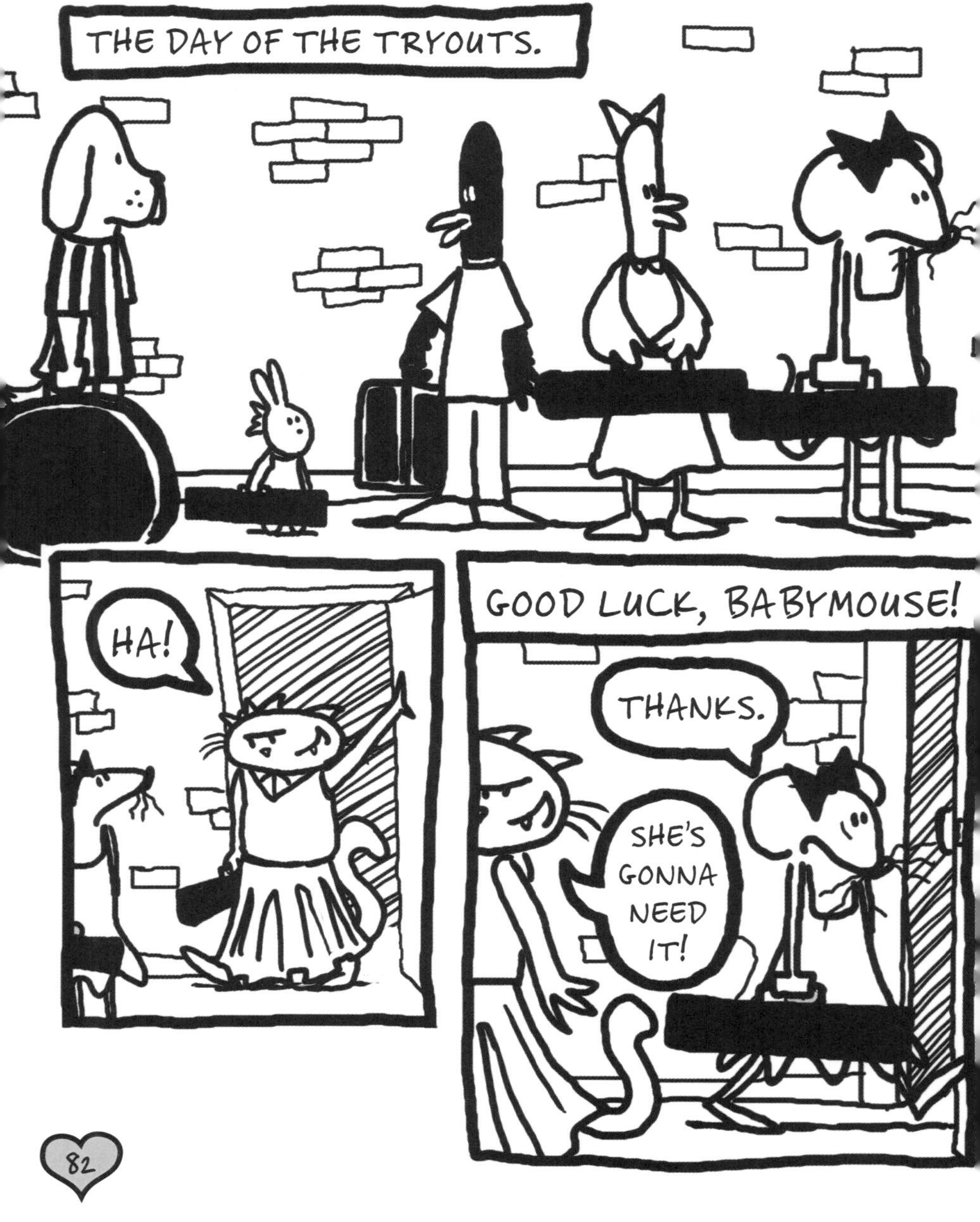
THE DAY OF THE TRYOUTS.
HA!
GOOD LUCK, BABYMOUSE!
THANKS.
SHE'S GONNA NEED IT!

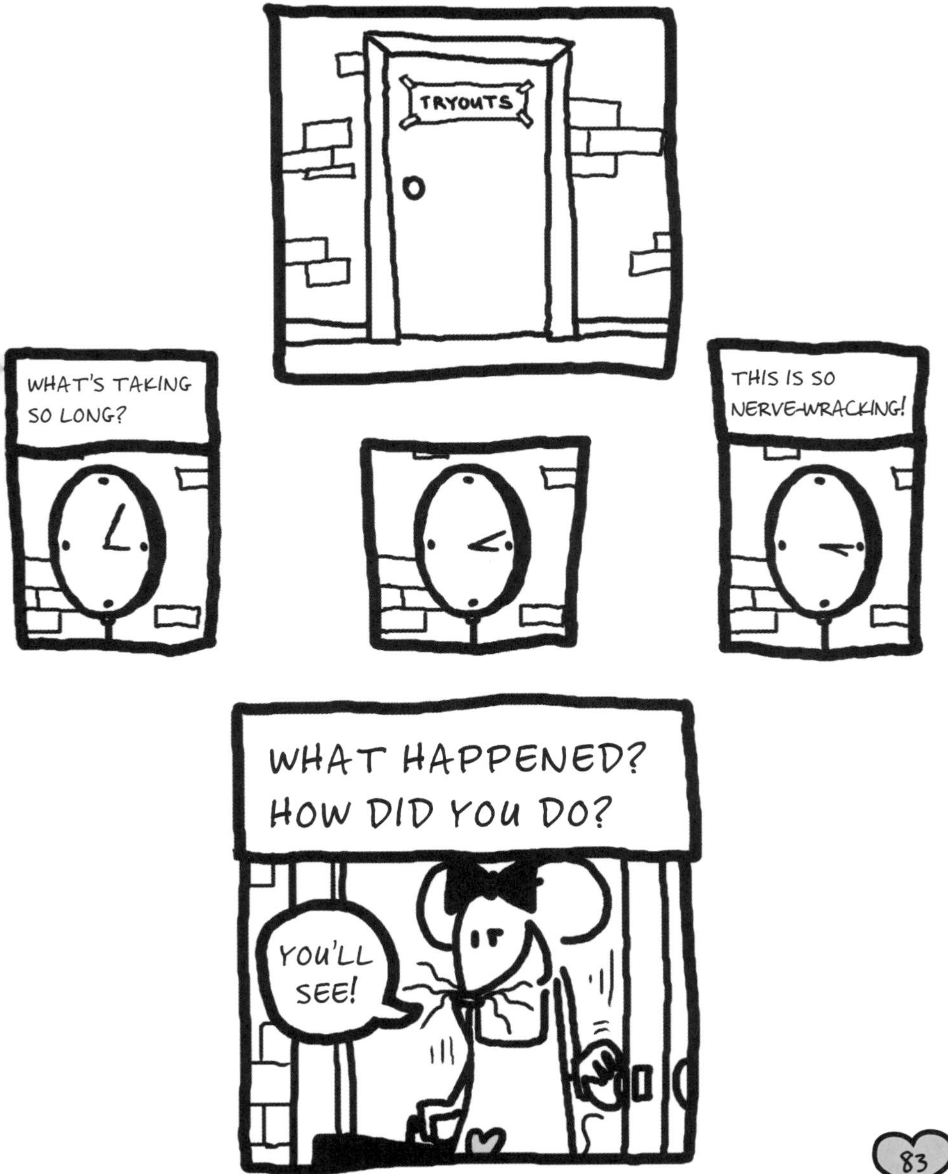
TRYOUTS
WHAT'S TAKING SO LONG?
THIS IS SO NERVE-WRACKING!
WHAT HAPPENED? HOW DID YOU DO?
YOU'LL SEE!

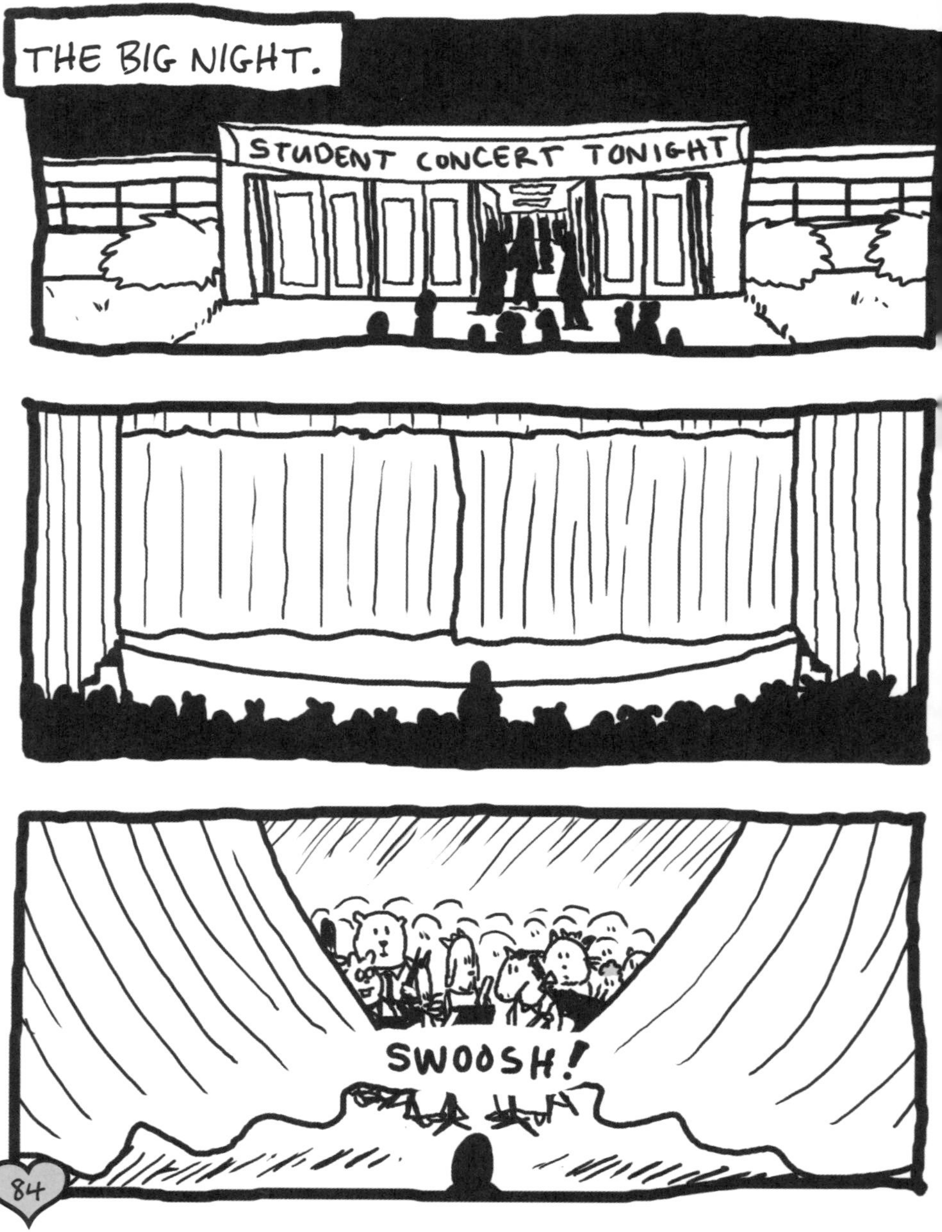
THE BIG NIGHT.
STUDENT CONCERT TONIGHT
SWOOSH!

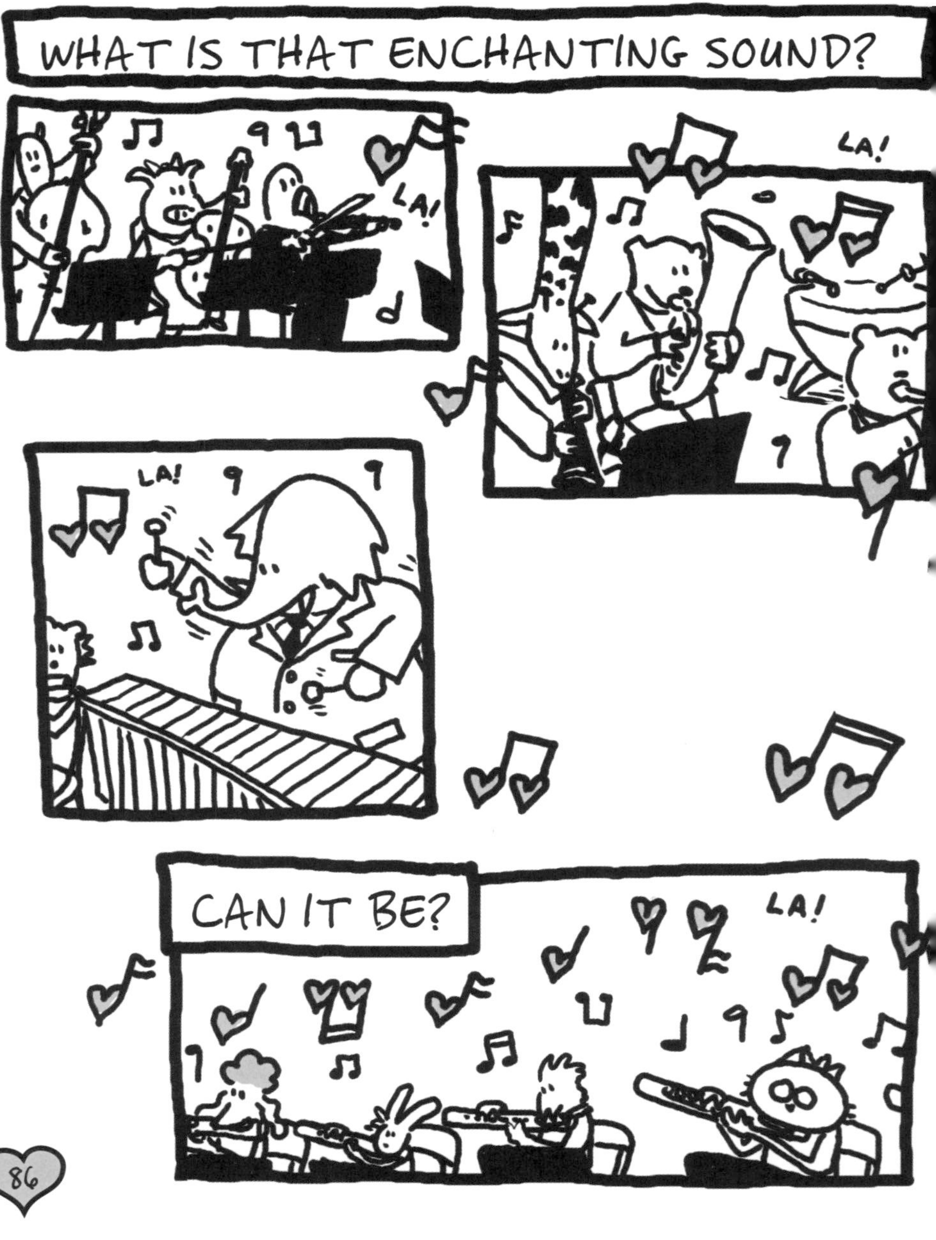

WHAT IS THAT ENCHANTING SOUND?
LA!
LA!
LA!
CAN IT BE?
LA!

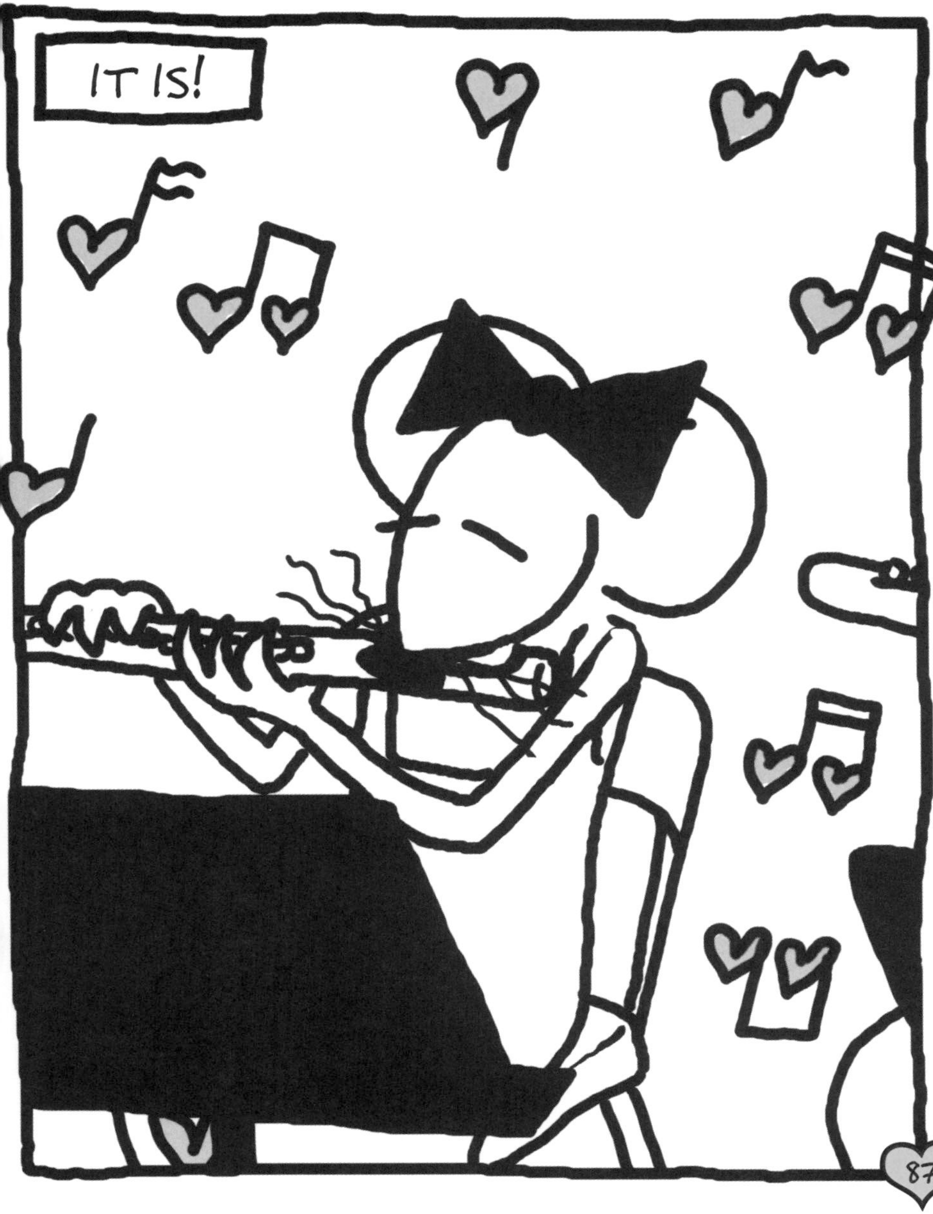
IT IS!

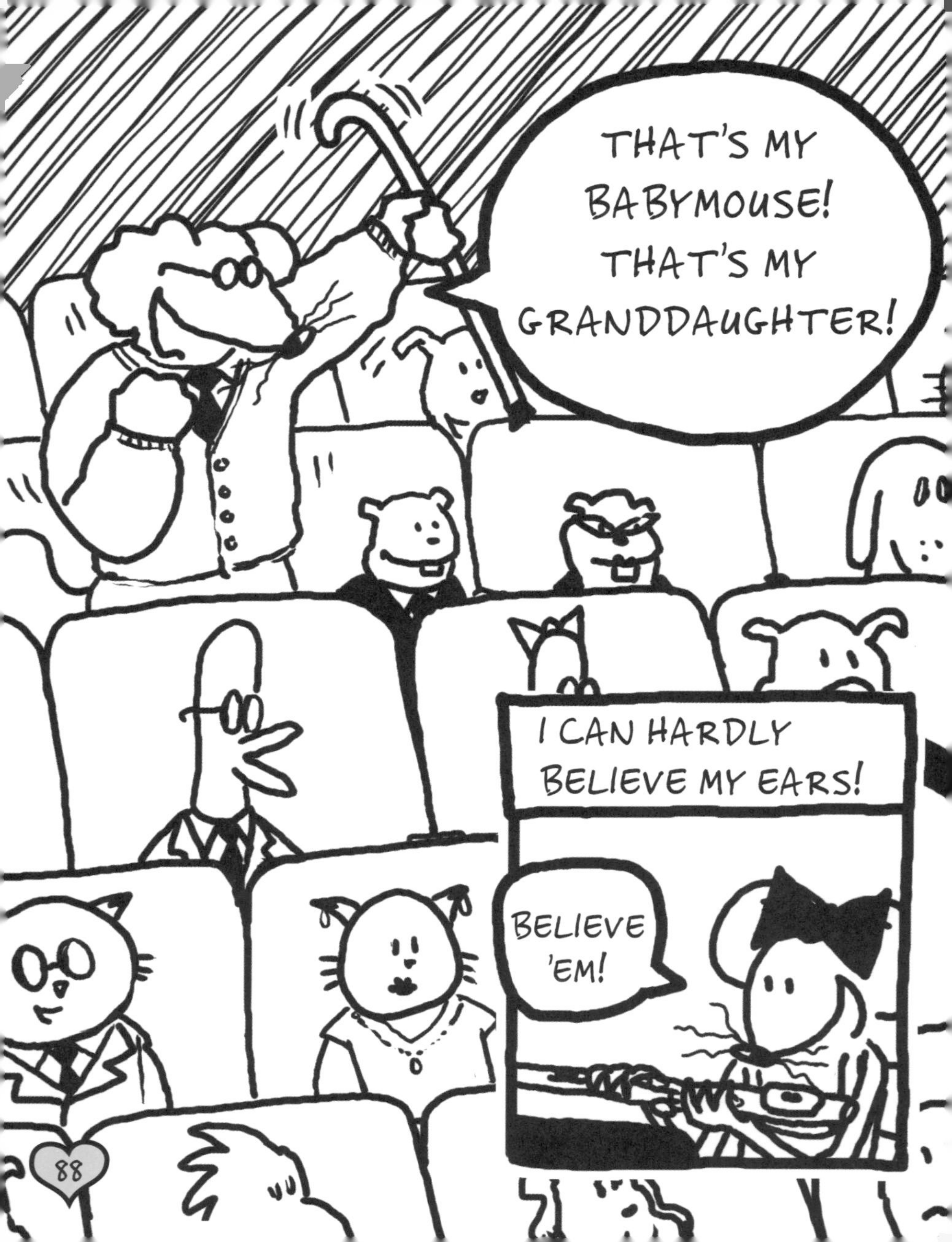
THAT'S MY BABYMOUSE! THAT'S MY GRANDDAUGHTER!
I CAN HARDLY BELIEVE MY EARS!
BELIEVE 'EM!

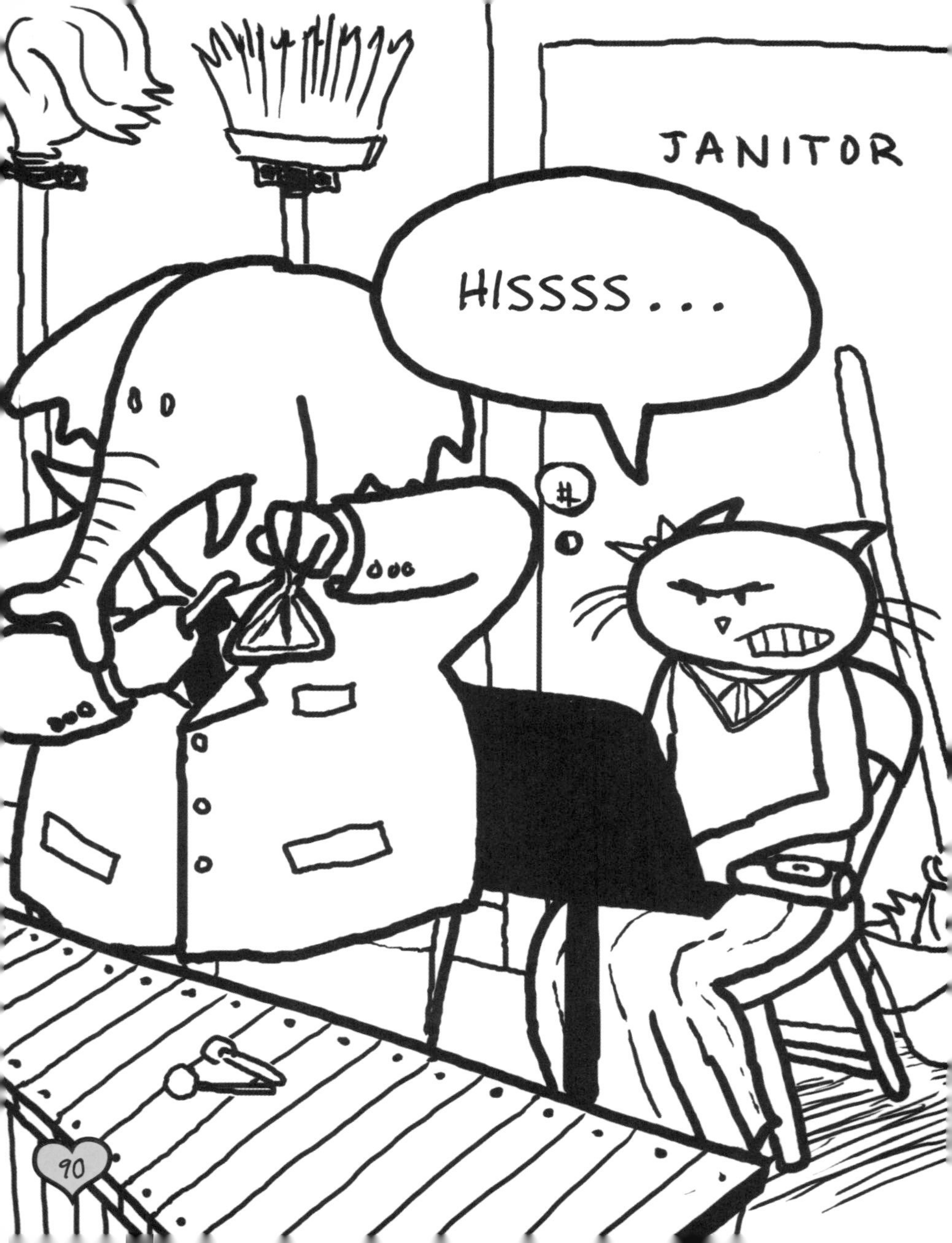
JANITOR
HISSSS . . .

NOT BAD, BABYMOUSE, BUT I DON'T THINK YOU'RE READY FOR A WORLD TOUR YET.

HEY! I DON'T SEE **YOU** PLAYING AN INSTRUMENT, BUSTER!

THANK YOU. THANK YOU VERY MUCH.

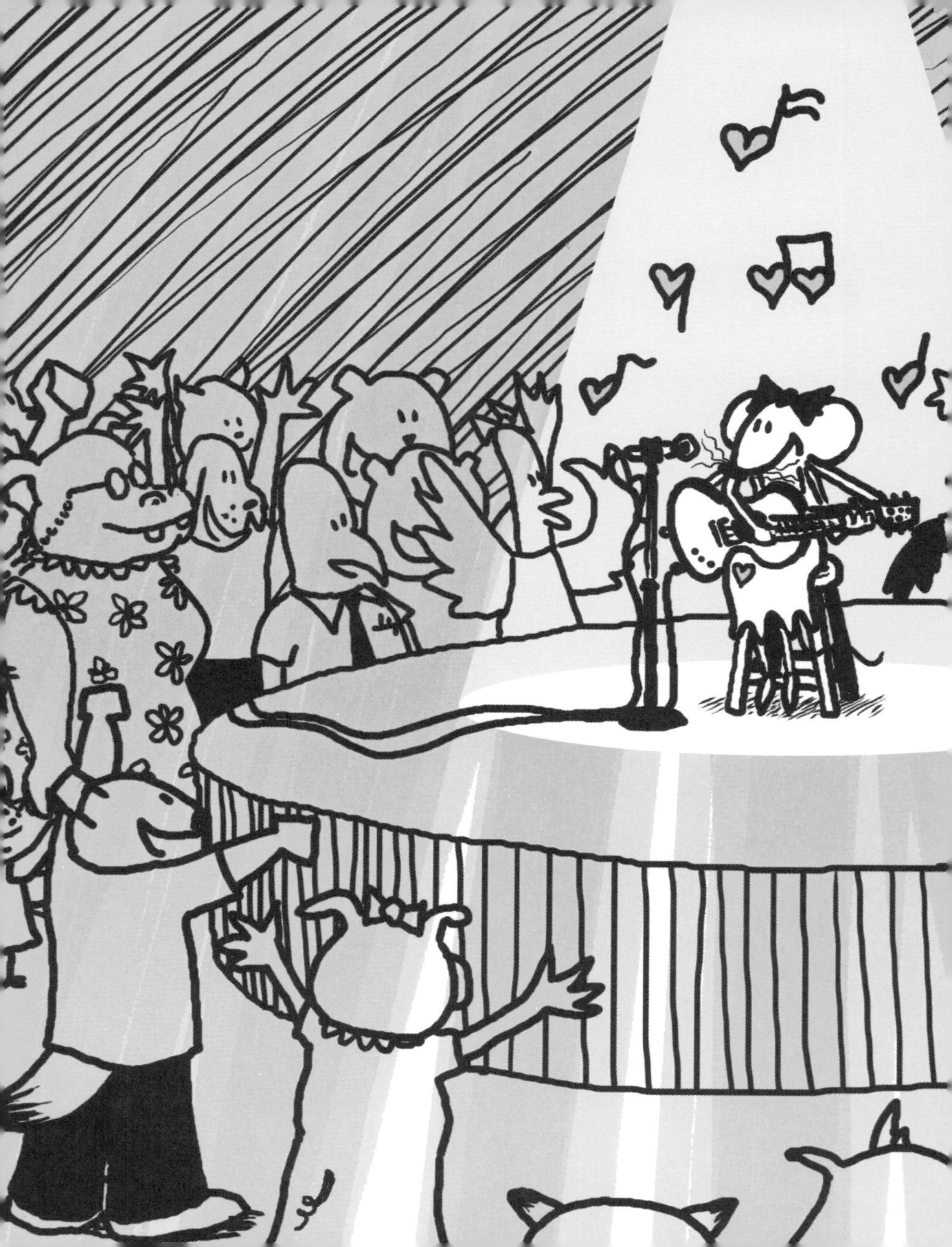

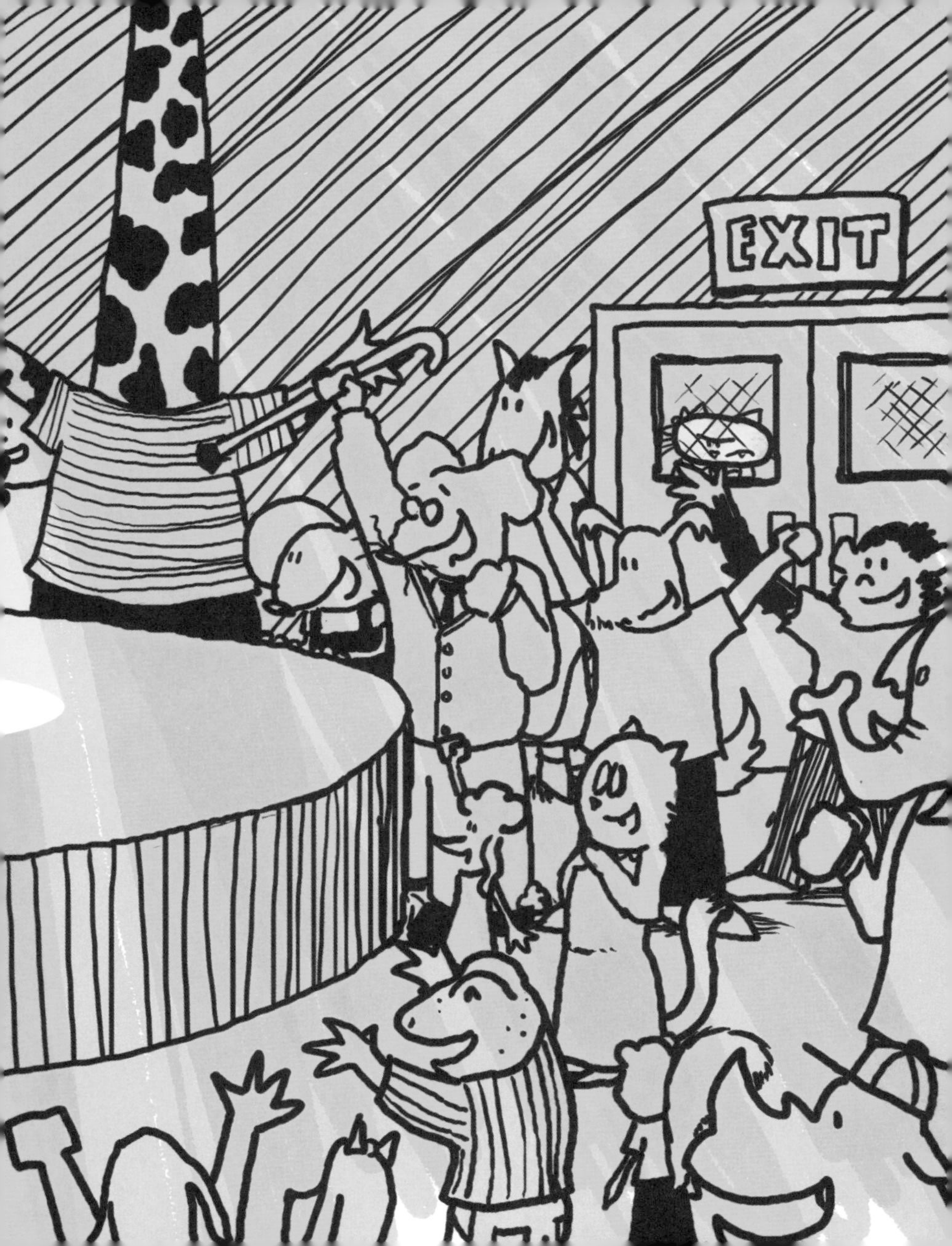
EXIT

BABYMOUSE BONUS!

• TIPS ON BEING A ROCK STAR •

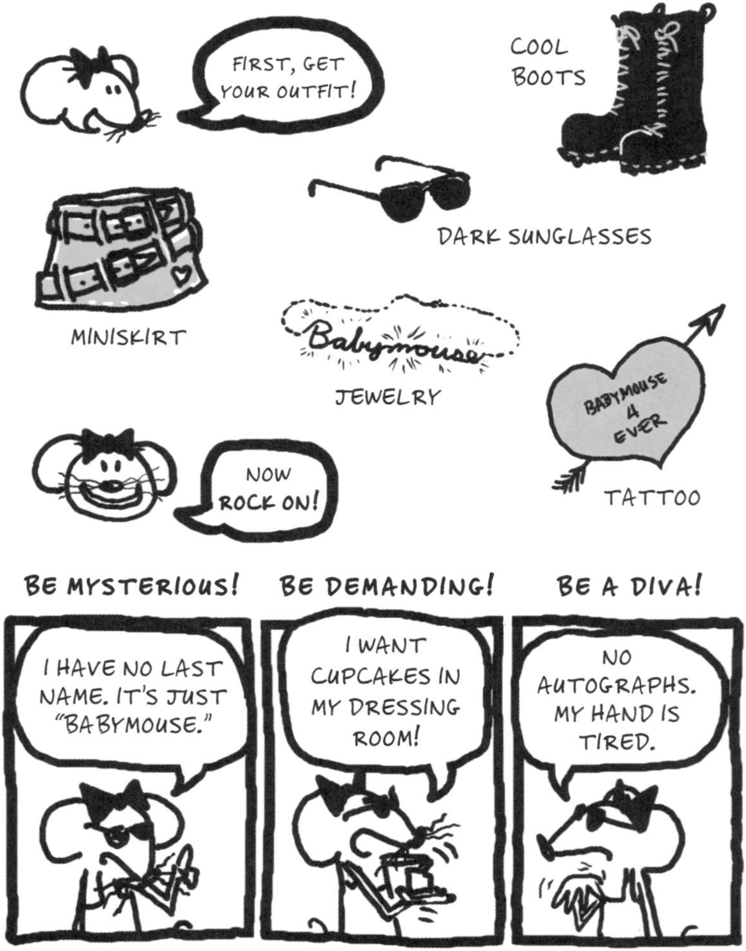
FIRST, GET YOUR OUTFIT!
COOL BOOTS
DARK SUNGLASSES
MINISKIRT
Babymouse
JEWELRY
BABYMOUSE 4 EVER
TATTOO
NOW ROCK ON!
BE MYSTERIOUS!
I HAVE NO LAST NAME. IT'S JUST "BABYMOUSE."
BE DEMANDING!
I WANT CUPCAKES IN MY DRESSING ROOM!
BE A DIVA!
NO AUTOGRAPHS. MY HAND IS TIRED.